SECRETS OF A PASTOR'S WIFE 3

BILLIE MIFF

Urban Aesop Presents

Copyright © 2021 by Billie Miff

All rights reserved.

No part of this book may be reproduced in any form or by any electronic or mechanical means, including information storage and retrieval systems, without written permission from the author, except for the use of brief quotations in a book review.

PROLOGUE

WHILE THE SEASONS CHANGE, SOME THINGS STAY THE same. The climate in the Andrews' household had been tumultuous over the past few months. With Chloe preparing for life as a college student, she had pretty much closed out the world around her. The one positive was her reconnect with Gabriel. After his return to school, seeing each other made it virtually impossible to keep them separated. Similar social circles caused them to be in each other's presence, as teenagers staying angry was hard to do.

Gabriel's gun shot wound to the leg was completely healed but instead of his strong confident gait, he had a slight yet noticeable limp. His hopes were that he could regain enough mobility to attempt training for basketball season. If he had any chance of getting a scholarship, he had to return to the form that had every high school team fearing to face him on the court and every recruiter salivating at the chance to watch him play. Game, the name he made famous, had a lot of supporters, people wanted to see him win, not just on the court but in life in general, none more loyal than Chloe. Carl wished he had supporters on his side. The tide in his life had drifted drastically. The extra marital affair allegations coupled with the estranged relationship with his son, Carl Jr., publicity for the budding young pastor had been all negative. As the head of his household, it had been equally as hard keeping his family in order. His wife, Sandra, was on the verge of making a critical decision regarding her own future. Leaving him was not out of the realm of possibilities.

Sandra, or Cookie as she had been affectionately known as by her friends, had her life to consider. She was striving to be the best mother she could be and that was becoming tougher with two daughters in their teens, heading in different directions. Her relationship was still strained with Chloe. Over the years it had gotten better but not where it should be between mother and daughter. She was getting ready for a new chapter in life; college was a big step, yet there were no woman to woman talks, no shopping trips to the mall that would naturally bond them, or even conversations about how men were supposed to treat women. Those were the instilling moments that were void in their lives. It wasn't like Cookie hasn't tried, its Chloe who has put the wall. She only lets in who she wants. Sometimes, her mother gets a glimpse of the inside and sometimes she doesn't, it all depends on the day and her mood.

It hurt Sandra to her heart to know her oldest daughter, though not biological, was about to leave the nest and enter into adulthood without them being closer. She found herself clinging tighter to Reecie, her 15 year old, hoping that she took heed to her teachings. Reecie's mind was very impressionable with everything that was going on around her. The tornado that surrounded her father, the longing she had for a sister-sister bond, and a loving relationship she was desperately trying to hold onto, all was etching a dysfunctional mindset, something that was unhealthy at her age. Sandra did everything she could to wrap her wings around her youngest and keep her from harm. However, eventually she would have to face the world head on, at that point it would be known whether she'd be ready. No one could predict how the events in the Andrews' home would turn out. With no true leadership, it would be difficult to keep the walls from crumbling. As long as there were secrets, there would be messy situations. Sandra was still holding onto a couple of secrets of her own. She just hoped her hand didn't get caught in the cookie jar before she would be able to clean her life up. All she ultimately wanted was happiness, she had to figure if she was going about it the right way.

CHAPTER ONE

Reecie

I SEE A LOT, I HEAR A LOT, I JUST DON'T SAY MUCH about anything. Whatever was happening with my mom and dad was not right. I notice other parents who are loving towards each other yet when I look at how my folks interact it gives me an example of how I don't want to be. They must think that children don't pick up on things but we do. We have a voice too and I guess its time for me to start using mine. Everyday when mom drops me off at school, I worry about her. I known its supposed to be the other way around and in her eyes it probably is but I can't help but worry. I've always had an innate connection with her which will pretty much be there forever. So when I see her mood change, it has an effect on me too. Today wasn't any different. We rode the whole way in silence, she didn't even hum along when one of her favorite gospels songs from Mary Mary came on the radio. Usually her melodic harmony makes it sound like she belongs in the group. And since I picked up singing from her, I would join in making us a group of angelic voices. The church choir doesn't do her justice because my momma can really sing. That uplifting sound wasn't there today and it disturbed me. Today there was no tune, no finger tapping on the steering wheel, just an uncomfortable void. I wasn't used to this side of her and I surely wasn't trying to get used to it now.

"What's wrong, momma?" I broke the icy silence. She paused before she spoke then decided to respond.

"What makes you think something's wrong, baby?" Guess she thought it was safe to answer a question with a question.

"You know I know you like a book, " I teased. "Remember I came out of that tummy of yours, spent nine months, eight hours and twenty seven minutes inside of you and it was very uncomfortable." She chuckled which means I got to her.

"And how do you know you were uncomfortable, young lady?" She countered but I wasn't gonna let her off the hook.

"I told you, I pay attention to a lot. A baby has to feel discomfort before it comes into the world."

"You are very wise, my dear."

"I believe you already knew that. Its also my job to look out for your well being."

"Oh it is? I didn't know that you had another job other than going to school, chores, dance at the church, and bible study." She had me there. But I still rebounded.

"Yes and watching out for you is in that list too." She just smiled knowing that I wasn't giving up. "Somebody has to, you know. So since we're on the subject of your wellbeing, how are you holding up?"

"Holding up? Did somebody die that I don't know about?"

"Your spirits dead, mom, if you want to know the truth. With all the things going on in dad's life, I'm sure some of it has to be affecting you in some way."

"Honestly, Reecie, I don't know what to think. His son contacted me the other day to speak." I was certainly shocked to hear that. I had my own feelings on that whole ordeal but now it was about her.

"And how did that go?"

"Don't know. I sent him to voice mail. I'm just not ready to deal with that issue at the moment. We still have some cleaning up to do around our home."

"I spoke to him." I mumbled out.

"Excuse me? You did what?" She looked at me as if she didn't hear what I said, but I know she did.

"We talked, mom." I repeated.

"And how did that conversation go?" There was a hint of attitude in her voice.

"Fine, I guess. He seemed nice. His issue was with daddy."

"What issue was that? I'm sure its not the same issues I have with your father."

"It sounded like he just wanted to be a part of a family. He seemed sad with all the time that was lost." Mom stared at the road as if she was trying to come up with the right words to say. I couldn't imagine how she viewed things. All these years not knowing about this man, then out of nowhere he just shows up, I could tell by her expression that she was at a loss, wondering how things would change.

"You know your father should've told us about this Carl guy, long ago."

"Carl Jr. is what he said his name was. They have the same name, mom, he has to be his son."

"So he says. Reecie, sometimes people aren't who they say they are." She explained.

"I don't get it. Why would someone pretend to be somebody they're not?" I was confused.

"People do things for different reasons. And I'm not saying that he's not your father's son, I'd just like to know the whole story before I let him into my life. And right now your father is not being completely honest about the situation." She went on and on about how things weren't adding up. "Trust is a huge thing" she said, her trust was in God, we as humans will change and alter facts to our liking. "We can't determine truth like that," she stated plainly. My truth is daddy got blindsided with the news and was as shocked as we were. Maybe momma had a point, there may be more to the story. We pulled up to my school's entrance and her mood changed to a more chipper one.

"Alright, sweetie, have a wonderful day. Your father

will be here to pick you up this afternoon." I was hoping my disappointment didn't show but it did.

"Aww, I thought you were coming back to get me?"

"I have a scheduled appointment I can't miss. I'm sorry baby." I was fine with her explanation. Just wish we had more time together. I knew if she could she would, so I wasn't too upset. After kissing her on the cheek, I exited. A couple of my friends met me at the entrance. Sasha, Joi and I girl talked while we headed to our lockers. High School was a hard transition coming from middle school where life seemed so simple. Socially, things were way more challenging, especially when phones were as necessary as calculators.

"Why is everyone looking at me so strange, snickering and stuff?" I asked

"We tried to be the first to tell you," Sasha said

"Tell me what?" Now I was worried. Like I didn't have enough to deal with outside of school.

"Girl, these folks look at their phones like they read the newspaper and right now your dad is front page news", Joi chided. She was always the bearer of bad news and on top of that she's a gossip queen herself. We get most of our dirt from her. I pulled out my phone from my book bag and went to SkoolChat, a social site this tech student came up with to connect students of high school ages at different schools. On the lead page were various stories about my daddy going viral.

"Pastor with Problems" was one of the headlines.

"Heads or Tails, Pastor doesn't know whether he's coming or going!"

"A Good Word or a Good Lie, which one do you believe?"

All these titles were aimed at slandering my father's name and credibility. I stepped in the crease of my open locker door and clicked on one of the stories. Perusing down, I viewed one person's distorted version of what they thought was the truth. After reading a few lines of obvious fiction, I thought back to what my mom just told me about how people will change things up for their own gratification.

"Pastor Carlton Andrews of the famed Victory in Faith Baptist Church is in a bit of hot water. With the swirling rumors of illegitimate family members, he is in serious jeopardy of losing the very church he spent valuable time building up. The congregation of loyal followers are on the verge of walking out, leaving him with no flock to lead. Imagine that, a herd of sheep running loose because of a misguided Shepherd. How can he be asked to keep his church family together when he can't even hold his own together? Answer that, Pastor, then maybe we will follow you."

I had read enough. People can be so cruel at the expense of gossip. The way they were slaughtering my dad ripped a hole in my heart. I know he has some problems, but who doesn't? And does his deserve to be aired out for the world to see? What will this do to my reputation as a student? Being a PK was hard enough without the drama, being related to the famous Pastor Andrews put me on the map, in a negative way.

"Don't worry, Reecie, it will blow over" Sasha tried to

console me as we walked to first period. Joi was still scrolling through the social site obviously amused by the various gossip. I guess she needed some new tea to add to her mix.

"Chile, please, this might last forever, like the Keith Sweat song!" She joked. Joi always had something witty to say and for the most part it was usually funny but not at my expense.

"Damn, girl, you don't spare nobody, do you? You ain't got no class," Sasha defended.

"I do have class, Biology in about five minutes," she guffawed, cracking herself up.

"Anyway," I said. "I'll catch up with y'all later" she was all into throwing shade and I didn't have time for that mess.

I found it hard to concentrate throughout the day with all that was going on. My life was taking a twisted turn and I wasn't even the cause. This definitely wasn't how I was trying to make my mark, I had a different outcome in mind about how my path would be. Everyone had scars, I just hoped these weren't the ones that were permanent. From class to class, I got looks of disgust. Every corner I turned I ran into someone I didn't know acting like they knew something about me and my family. Opinions were already formed like what was circulating in the rumor mill actually defined who I was. I have great aspirations of one day going to a performing arts college where my dancing abilities can be enhanced, marketed, then turned into a profession. The classes and after school activities were just a stepping stone to my dream. Although the things these kids were saying could be damaging to the average teen, I would be affected if I considered myself average, which I don't.

After school I waited out front for my daddy to show up. For the first time in a while I was actually embarrassed to be picked up by him. I'm glad his Mercedes wasn't recognizable by sight or otherwise his arrival may have caused a scene. As of now, no one knew who was coming to get me. Sasha and Joi always waited with me and the assumption was that my mom was coming. I didn't let them know otherwise. I wasn't worried about Sasha but Joi didn't know how to let things rest. I was seriously thinking about reevaluating our friendship, she just hasn't done anything detrimental enough to distance myself. That's today, there's always tomworrow, the jury is still out. Daddy pulled up a little late but it was alright in my book. He was still daddy to me and I wasn't taking score of the rights and wrongs like everybody else. My family getting its closeness back was what's important to me, everything else could catch the bus. The tint on dads car helped me to escape without questions, I only wished life could have tinted windows for me to hide behind sometimes.

"How was school today, baby girl?" He asked without a clue as to what I'd been through.

"Fine." My answer was short.

"Just fine? Nothing new and exciting?" If he only knew.

"Normal teenage gossip, that's all."

CHAPTER TWO

Adrian

THE MONTHLY COUNTDOWN TO MY RELEASE SEEMED like the hardest time yet. It was bad enough I was waiting on a parole decision, that in itself meant I had to be on my best behavior. I can control myself, that wasn't the issue, it was the challenge of avoiding the outside distractions. It's easy to have a "stay out of trouble" mindset, but there were times where trouble seems to locate you.

Ever since I received the notice that I would soon be free from the prison system, its taken everything in my power to keep my sanity. So much to think about, even more to consider, over fifteen years on the inside, the outside world will seem like shock treatment. I'm just glad that over the years I've been able to hold my own and not allow this time to suck me in. I've seen a lot of guys lose it in here. Either through homosexuality or mental illness, some chose alternate paths to cope. It takes a stable man, with a stable mind to withstand this type of environment.

It helps to have good people in your corner, the people you associate with can play a major part in the journey. That's why I kept my circle small. Preacher Man was my closest partner and I could actually consider him a friend. Its more than what I can say I had on the street, family was a priority whether they were there for me or not.

Doing time helps you to reflect. I think a lot about how things were fifteen years ago. If I could do it all over again, how would I do it differently? Who knows? In some ways, I wouldn't change a thing, then in other instances I want to go back with what I know now and do life better. To be able to change the past is a no brainer, however when I look at how time changed me, how can I be sure life would be any better had I not come to prison. I may sound crazy but prison could have really saved my life. I know for some in here, it definitely saved theirs.

My family really doesn't know this version of Adrian Upshaw. When I first started my sentence I received a lot of support from family. When I was doing county jail time, everyone could see the love. Officers would come up to me and tell me how blessed I was to always have visitors. Mail would come in like clockwork, it didn't matter if it was a card, letter, or a money order for commissary, it was the attention everyone saw. Over time things started to change. Once I got to prison, the visits dwindled, becoming less of a priority in peoples lives. Family became busier, it felt like I had been forgotten about.

I remember my brother, who is a few years older than me, would come and see me two and three times a week. It had gotten to be routine and his visits something I had come to rely on as a part of doing time. Then, out of nowhere, they just stopped. He had a new wife, a child on the way, when I first got locked up. One day I got a letter from him stating his wife was having serious issues with him coming to see me so much. He told me everything she said, raw and uncut. I developed a hatred towards her without even considering how she must be feeling. Her main point was that he had a life to live and I had mine. "It wasn't your fault he wasted his life and went to prison", she said to him, taking a heated shot at me. I believe she convinced him because he sure pulled back from visiting altogether. I resented her for a long time because of that and had angst towards my brother for falling weak and siding with her instead of his own flesh and blood.

Time has a way of placing negative thoughts in your head. I was bitter towards them both but time helped me to change my heart. Since then our relationship has been a little more amicable, my brother even has brought his family to see me. It felt good to make amends face to face.

When I was young, my brother Addison was who I looked up to. As with all big brother/little brother relationships, we fought, I used to steal from him, wear his clothes, follow him around, the normal behavior. The love was there between us, we just had to go through our growing pains. Overall, Addison was a positive influence on me. He never got into any trouble, always a good student and a better athlete. I believe that's where my competitiveness derived from, through sports. That will to never give up and fight against all odds was instilled in me from my brother. Growing up watching him on the football field showed me what grit and determination was all about. I always admired the toughness he displayed, not to mention the good sportsmanship that won him numerous awards and accolades. It was easy to consider Addison a role model.

With our father passing away at an early age, Addison was the only male figure I had in my life. He impressed upon me to always take care of our mother because we were all she had. Throughout his high school years I could see his priorities change, he definitely practiced what he preached. His whole focus became about mom. Even at his football games, which she never missed, he made it a point to acknowledge her especially when he scored. Addison would spot her in the stands and blow her a kiss as a testament to her undying support. After the games, as we walked back to the car, I would carry his helmet but mom would have his Letterman's jacket draped around her slender shoulders.

There were times I was envious of their relationship. My youth wouldn't allow me to understand that he was just being an example of how a son was supposed to treat his mother; how a man was supposed to treat a woman. Looking back I saw ways where I could've done more, been a better son. My brother, Addison was the apple of her eye, me I guess I was like a sour grape.

Mom did all she could to hold strong during my time away. When she would come and visit, which wasn't often, it took everything in me to keep from crying when she got ready to leave. Part of me wanted to let the tears flow but I withheld my true emotions fearing that the surrounding inmates would view me as being weak. She would look at me with loving eyes yet I could see the hurt I was causing her. My heart ached to be able to do something to ease her pain, to do something to change what had happened. After so many trips to prison I could see it wearing on her. It was weakening her from the inside out. Then to watch her leave knowing I wasn't walking out with her, made it that much harder. I'd much rather inflict myself with pain just to spare her but unfortunately that's not how life works. Sometimes our choices bring consequences and those consequences affect other people, my mother was one of those people.

On the inside, I didn't realize just how many lives I had affected. The world spins at a thousand miles per hour but when you're locked up, lives comes to a screeching halt. That's when I sit and think about the ones I love the most. Now that I'm close to returning to the outside world, I have to reevaluate my life and figure out how I'm going to turn things around. My hope is that my mom and brother receive me with an open mind. I'm coming out a different man and I need them to see the new me.

"Adrian, you seem different today like something has come over you. Don't tell me the church services are taking their effect on you?" Preach jested noticing a change

"That may not be too far from the truth. On the real, I'm just getting my mind together. Working on flushing out all this negative around here, trying to fill it with positive."

"I hear ya, bro, more power to you. That's not easy to do with these dudes," he stated truthfully.

Preach didn't know what was going on with me and my parole. Its not that I'm keeping it from him, he's my partner and all that, its just too soon to put that energy out there. Haters come in many forms and I don't want anybody stealing my joy. No disrespect to Preach but this news I plan on keeping to myself for a while.

"Hey, on another note, we're probably due to get a bunch of new arrivals tomorrow. Carter, who works up there in ID said he saw a list and they're all Hispanics."

"All Hispanics? That's odd. Wonder why that is?"

"He said he heard the transfer Sgt., the one who transports from spot to spot, spoke about a mini riot that broke out at Stanley Prison, that new joint out by the Eastern Shore. It was some sort of race war and the Hispanics were the minority. I guess it was easier to round them up rather than separate the blacks."

"Was it gang related?" I asked out curiosity, it didn't really matter one way or the other.

"With Hispanics, you have to treat them like a gang. You known they roll together. They ain't like us, they don't tend to fight each other. I hate to state the obvious but I'm just saying."

The system was getting worse by the day. Violence was at an all time high, some people in here have war stories like Afghan war veterans. This is our battle ground, its taken seriously.

"Why are they shipping them here? I though we were housing inmates with lower security levels?"

"Well, that's the thing, it turns out that the Warden here agreed to accept them."

"So now we have to be prepared for an increase in violence on our compound?" Preached seemed concerned.

"Not really. From my experience, Hispanics don't usually bother unless they're bothered. They generally don't initiate unless they're provoked."

"How do the incident jump off at the other spot?"

"From what Carter says, it escalated when a black inmate was attacked on the walk by a number of Hispanics as retaliation for something someone else did." I was shocked

"No way, an innocent bystander?"

"Yup, and get this, they say he was on his way to counseling to sign his going home papers. He got caught at the cross gate where they stabbed him multiple times. It turns out that the lady who works the electronic gate panicked and didn't open the gate in time."

"Preach, for someone who doesn't know much about the situation, you sure got a detailed report as if you were the lead investigator. How do you do it?" I asked laughing.

"Shoot, Inmate.com will have you in the know, asap." He joked back "I'm plugged in like a socket!"

"I see."

After hearing him recount those events, that just confirmed my notions about putting my business out there. People don't care whether you're trying to get out or working on getting yourself together. If its not benefitting them immediately, then you don't matter a bit. Instead of someone being happy for you having a good outlook, they'd rather be the one who dampens your spirit. Its sad but its true. Misery truly loves good company. The same could be said about the outside world, the same place I'm desperately trying to get back to.

CHAPTER THREE

Cookie

REECIE WAS GROWING UP SO FAST. SOMETIMES SHE acts like she's the mother and I'm her daughter. I'd be a fool to think that what Carl and I are going through wasn't taking a toll on her. She's in those critical teenage years where she's supposed to be learning about womanhood. However, our problems are a little too grown for her to be dealing with at this time. I want her growth to be natural even when what we're going through is so unnatural.

I knew it was time to make an attempt to come to some common ground with Carl, if not for us, for Reecie's sake.

"Carl, can we talk?" There was an eerie silence before his voice came through the phone.

"Oh, so now you want to talk. Sandra, if I recall correctly, I tried to get you to talk with me a few days ago. You acted as if coming home, to my home, was too much to ask, like the worst idea ever!" Here he goes with the dramatics.

"Carl, trust me, if you only knew....it really wasn't a good time." I tried to avert the subject altogether but I should've known better, should've known Carl better.

That day had my mind in a whirlwind. All I could think about was safety, my daughter's, my husband's, especially my own. When I looked out the window and saw those thugs in our neighborhood, it had me shook. They were on the prowl checking plates. I knew what they were looking for, I just regretting not going with my first mind and parking my car in the garage. When one of them eyed my tags, my heart dropped to my stomach. My thoughts raced faster than light speed. I left the window trying to devise a plan, coming up with nothing at all. What if they come to the door? What do I say? I couldn't hide because my car was there, that wouldn't be smart. Adrian calling scared the living daylights out of me. Although I was glad to hear his voice, his timing couldn't have been worse. I didn't want to let on to what was happening, no need to have him worried in there, there wasn't much he could do anyway.

Without raising suspicion, I hung up with Adrian abruptly so I could decide what to do next. In my mind, I wanted him there but I knew trust wasn't possible so there was no need to wrap him up in my drama. When I went back to the window, a pair of eyes were focused my way. I believe the motion of the blinds gave me away. Quickly, I ducked out of sight. I was stuck between curiosity and fear, curiosity had won the battle. Putting my brave girl panties, I peered out one more time, to my surprise the man who was looking my way was now on the phone walking towards the vehicle that carried them there.

My heart regained normal cadence temporarily as I tried to regain my composure. Carl had called back but I sent it to IGNORE.

"Where have you been? Your daughter has been asking about you." I stated with enough black girl attitude to give him a rise.

"What is it to you? And why do you even care, Sandra?" I wanted to say something smart to rebut his comment but I refrained.

"Your daughter was worried about you." He didn't say anything. "I was worried about you." He let out a puff of air, which I ignored. "Why didn't you come home?"

"Look, Sandra, I needed some time to myself. I'm not gonna lie, you made me feel rejected."

"You were drinking too, weren't you?" His silence told me his truth

"What does it really matter? You caring about me or what I do doesn't really seem genuine to me." Why did this have to go in this direction. He always had a way of making himself the victim. My purpose for the call was to discuss our daughter Reecie, in particular. Chloe was in her own lane, acting like she didn't have a care in the world about what was going on under our roof. Her mind was on boys and school, in that order. Gabriel had decided to show interest again which brightened her outlook on life. I questioned his intentions with her in my mind but didn't act on it, no need to push the panic button too early. I kept my eyes on him though, bullying was more her father's thing.

"Are you at the church? I could meet with you there if you like?" I was really trying, even changing my tone.

"Yeah, I'm here. OK. Whenever is cool."

I ended Carl's unenthused ass phone call. Someone had to man-up in the situation, I thought it would at least be the MAN. Speaking of a man, I needed to return Adrian's call from the other day. I was kind of short with him and it certainly wasn't his fault. Maybe hearing about was going on his world would be a pleasant change. Imagine that, I'm actually interested in a man and his prison lifestyle. And I'm not mad at myself at all.

The phone rang a few times more than usual, then it went to voicemail. "Well, I tried" I said to myself out loud. In the next instance, I saw his name light up on my screen, and on my face, unconsciously, for that matter.

"Hello there" my tone was even with a hint of excitement.

"What's up, you? How are things going with you, Cookie?" It was nice to hear my name come from his voice, nickname and all.

"I'm good and you?"

"Maintaining, working to keep my sanity in here."

"Oh yeah, what's really going on?"

"You're really interested?" He sounded surprised.

"Sure I am. My world is so....agh! I need a change of scenery so to speak." I explained.

He started by bring me up to speed on then day to day events in his area. As he detailed everything, I found myself on the edge of my seat, listening to every word. It was almost like watching a movie, before we knew it two hours had passed. I was on the couch flipping channels. I had completely forgotten that I was supposed to meet with Carl at the church. For some reason I was fully content doing me, he would eventually come home then we could talk then. Chloe was floating back and forth in the kitchen phone to her ear. Reecie was busy on her laptop filling her brain with the latest dance craze. What I didn't realize was that it almost 11:30 and Carl still hadn't come home yet.

Adrian had me smiling from ear to ear. Of course we had to pause from time to time so he could check out his scene, making sure things were safe. Life on the inside had a story line of its own. He mentioned names like Scooby, Preacher Man, Clepto, Richie Rich, all these guys were like characters in a motion picture. The way he speaks about those guys like they're family.

"I have something I want to tell you." His voice change an octave which sent my stomach into knots. His voice was already sexy as hell but when it went lower it did something to me.

"I hope its not anything bad." I said trying to soften any blow.

"Actually, its all good. I'm coming home soon." I

heard Adrian loud and clear yet I couldn't mouth my response.

"That's great!" I said rather casually.

"Maybe you didn't hear me, I said I'm coming home. I'm getting out on parole." It took a minute for it to register. My first thought was, what was I gonna do now? It was all good when we were doing the phone thing. Now he was talking a real, in person thing. I wasn't ready to hear this news, good or not.

"Wow, baby!" That slipped out but I didn't even feel ashamed. "That's great news. When did you find out?" I was excited for him, that was for sure.

"A little over a week ago. You're actually the first person I've told. Not even my family."

"Not even your mother or brother?"

"Nope. Not yet. The timing hasn't been right."

"What's wrong with the time? This is your mom we're talking about, I know how you feel about her." I was concerned.

"Its not about their timing, its mine around here. I don't need these dudes in my business. Haters are alive and kicking in here!"

"Oh." Was all I could muster up. " I guess you know what's best in there."

If I had news like that, coming home after fifteen years away, incarcerated, I don't think I would want the world to know. It was understandable to keep something like that under wraps, I could only imagine the level of jealousy among him.

"Yeah, I have to be careful."

"How do you feel? Scared? Nervous? Anxious?"

"I guess all of the above, and then some. I still haven't wrapped my head around it yet. It's a new reality."

"I can't imagine what you must be thinking about. I'm just happy for you, Adrian."

"Did you just call me, baby?" I thought he missed that.

"Ahh....yes, I guess I did. Didn't think you caught it though."

"Its cool, I like hearing your real emotions."

"And how do you know that was my emotions coming out?"

"Because it was natural, like the first time our eyes met. Like our first conversation, smooth with no hitches."

"It was wasn't it? Our talks have always been easy." I agreed.

"So my question to you is, where do we go from here?" That was the question in was dreading to answer. And he hit me in the gut like a sucker punch with it. Truthfully, I never thought we would get to this point.

"My friend, that is not an easy one to answer. Its hard to say where we go from here when I'm not sure exactly where I'm at."

"I know where you're at, the same place you've been for years, stuck in a situation that needs to be fixed." He hit me with a heavy dose of reality.

"And what exactly do you expect me to do about it, Adrian?"

"Are you open to suggestions or was your question rhetorical?" His intelligence always had me questioning whether this man was actually incarcerated.

"I'm looking for help, Sir. I'm sitting here in a house that's not mine, with two girls that love their daddy very much. The whole situation is complex."

"It has been since the day I met you and has been many years before, according to our talks. You say the girls love him, which I expect but what about you?"

"What about me?" I knew where he was going with his line of questioning, I guess I just didn't want to face the truth, his truth.

"Do you love him, Cookie?" There it was. Blunt. Direct.

"Let me put it to you as plain as I can, yes I love him...as the provider and father of my children but our love for each other as husband and wife has long past gone for me. I can't speak for Carl and I won't attempt to. He has his load to bear and I have mine. We are going in different directions." It felt good to get that off my chest.

"So if I were to tell you that I plan to look you up when I leave here, what would you say?" He went straight for the throat.

"I want to say that's what I look forward to. My head says be wise in our decisions."

"What does your heart say, Cookie?'

"My heart.....my heart says that I've already fallen for you."

CHAPTER FOUR

Carl

Father God, I am a sinner, unwashed and unclean in your sight. I have a special responsibility as a messenger to deliver your word to your children. Although, I've tried to do that with all my energy, all my soul, and all my conviction, I still feel like I failed you. My spirit is empty, O Lord, empty to the point where the pits of my insides seem hollow. I humbly ask for your forgiveness. You say in your word that you desire a contrite heart, my prayer is for mercy. With all the events that have come forth of late, only you know the truth. Its only you I can confess my transgressions. You and only you can clean up this mess that I'm in. Please, O Lord, don't forsake me any longer. Rescue me.

    I got up off my knees at the alter, my eyes still moist when I opened them. The sanctuary that I used to fill every Sunday was now empty. The area where our glorious choir would sing melodious hymns was now void of the heavenly voices that resonated across the church. The pulpit where all the powerful messages were delivered, transforming lives, looked like a different place to me. It used to be a place where I felt most comfortable, where I had the most control, yet now I've been weakened and don't feel worthy to even stand there.

"Its OK, Pop, I feel your pain." A hand touched my shoulder in a comforting way. At first I welcomed it then I turned to see who it was and cringed.

"What are you doing here?" It was kind of cold to address my son in such a way but considering feelings wasn't at the top of my priority list.

"Relax, Pop, I thought your church was open to everybody...well, I'm everybody!" He stated with a huge grin.

"First of all," I said standing to look him in the eye. "This is not my church, this place belongs to the Almighty God. I'm merely a vessel for the Lord."

"Shoot, I can't tell with all the signs and pictures of you around here, the Great and Wonderful Pastor Carlton Andrews," he expressed with grand exaggeration.

"There are no such signs and you know it," I corrected.

"Ok , maybe not, but there are plenty of pictures of you, that's for sure. Not so many of the First Lady, I might add. How's she doing, by the way?"

"Why do you ask?"

"Shouldn't I be concerned about her as well? She is my stepmother, right?"

"Wrong." I answered flatly. His whole facial expression changed

"What do you mean?"

Maybe I wasn't willing to accept what was becoming my truth. Was God playing a cruel joke on me, sending this Carl Jr. a constant reminder of just how twisted my life is? I had to admit, when in looked into his eyes I saw my strong genes reflecting back at me. It was too much to digest at the moment. In wasn't ready for someone to barge their way into my life, a life that is already in disarray. I feel like I'm losing my wife, my daughter's respect, my congregation's loyalty, and worst of all, my sanity.

"Look, Carl, I just need some time to sort some things out. I'm am mess right now, can't you see? This is supposed to be my safe haven and yet I feel like a stranger. I've been closed towards you for no reason. My stress level is up to here and I'm not used to being this out of control."

"Dad, you need to let it go."

"Let it go? How? I'm sure you've heard or read what these people have said about me."

"You think you're the first person somebody has said something about?" We took a seat in one of the pews and I just listened. "You are not a Super-Pastor, able to withstand insults and allegations without so much as a scratch. No, you're human and subject to go through some shit." My eyes widened when I heard him curse. "Oops, my bad, I am in church. See what I mean, nobody is perfect. You make a mistake, ask for forgiveness, then move forward."

I sat there quiet for a minute or so, pondering what Carl just told me. I'm there for so many people. I give advice to troubled teens, visit the sick in the hospital, even counsel couples that are struggling to stay together but I didn't realize how much I needed someone to give it to me straight. I always thought I had the power to fix my own problems, because I had a direct line to God. It took for my son to tell me how incomplete I am without help from others.

"What is it that you want from me? I believed I've asked you that before. This time, I'm asking sincerely. You're here for a reason, obviously."

"Well, if you think its about your money, that's definitely not it," he chuckled. "I've seen your house and you're no Creflo Dollar for sure." Now that for me to laughing and felt good to release an emotion other than anger. There's a certain joy that comes from laughing. It can break down walls, calm savage waters and changes moods. Mine was changing by the second.

"Where are you staying, Carl?"

"I'm at this extended stay hotel. Its paid up for a week, after that who knows. My little savings is dwindling fast, so I'm hoping to find some work soon." My wheels were turning trying to come up with a plan. Staying with us was not a solution, that would only add more issues but finding work could help the situation.

"What kind of work do you do?"

"I'm pretty good with my hands. You know, taking things apart, putting it back together. Plumbing, carpentry, electrical, things like that."

"Cars?"

"I tinker around, wouldn't say I'm an expert."

"OK." Was all I said.

"What do you have in mind, dad?"

"Just thinking." I could sense his hopes rising and I didn't want to make any promises. He didn't push either.

"Well, if you come up with something, I'll be around. At least I can catch you for Sunday services, right?"

"If my congregation hasn't left me." I said jokingly but there was a sense of seriousness to my tone.

"One thing about lost sheep, they never forget where home is."

On my way home, I reflected on my conversation with Carl, my son. My son. It was strange hearing it roll off my tongue. He was quite insightful and had a generally good spirit. After talking with him, my spirits were lifted also. There had to b something I could do for him, but what? Until I come up with something concrete I'd just keep encouraging him. That's a step in the right direction towards being a good father, something he's been missing.

When I walked in the door, I immediately noticed something peculiar. Sandra was seated comfortably on the sofa, then a sudden shift in her movement made her body tense up when I looked at her. I didn't say anything but it appeared like she was trying to conceal her phone. Guilt has a way of rearing its ugly head when you least expect it. The corner of her phone was still visible to me, I never let on that I saw something suspicious.

"Hey," I said in my customary tone.

"Hello," she answered back emotionless.

"I thought you were coming to the church to talk?"

"Time got away from me, before I knew it, here you come through the door."

"Oh" is all I chose to say to that.

I went over and spoke to Reecie, who was busy looking up something on the Internet. I kissed her on the cheek then went upstairs and took a shower. Chloe was in her room doing what teen girls do, talk on the phone. When I got out and put some clothes on, I knocked on her door and motioned for her to come downstairs. It was time for a family meeting.

I was already down in the living room when Chloe came slinking down the stairs like this was the last thing on earth she wanted to do.

"Reecie, can you come here for a minute, I want to talk to you guys. Chloe have a seat by your mother." She did reluctantly.

"I had a heart to heart with God today at the church. There are a number of things that have me burdened down, especially with all the rumors that are circulating." I noticed Sandra roll her eyes in disinterest. "Is there something you'd like to comment on, Sandra?" I guess she didn't like being put on the spot in front of her children.

"Rumors, Carl? Do you really want to address this right now? In front of the girls?"

"Actually, yes, people think I'm hiding something."

"You hid a son from us, for God's sake!" She blurted out.

"I can't hide what I didn't know about," I countered fully ready for anything she threw at me. This wasn't supposed to be a shouting match but she was turning it into one. "Madeline, Carl's mother, who I was with for a brief period before you, we had sex one time, literally. At the time, my life values were changing and I felt like what we were doing wasn't right. To put it plain, we were unequally yoked. Having sex with someone I wasn't married to didn't make sense."

"But you had unprotected sex with this woman before you decided to rethink your values." She gave me her sarcasm. I gave her truth back.

"Yes. I was young and foolish. Hell, sue me, Sandra." Chloe smiled while Reecie put her hand over her mouth. "Anyway, our relationship fizzled fast when our differences became more pronounced. We went about our respective lives not knowing that a few months later she would be pregnant with my child."

"And you guys never had anymore contact?" That was Chloe interjecting which i was glad. I wanted them to be involved in the conversation, this wasn't just about Sandra and I, it was a family thing.

"She moved away, from what I heard. I got the details from walking with Carl."

"So you've been talking with your son?" Sandra was

still in the shade business, it was OK, I wasn't going to stoop to her level.

"Yes, in fact we talked for a while this evening at the church. That's what I was doing while waiting for you. But I see you were preoccupied." I shot a look at her phone that she now knew was visible. Her expression and mood calmed.

"Dad, what about this stuff all over the Internet about you? I saw some more gossip today." Reecie said out of pure concern.

"That's all it is, baby, just gossip." I could tell Chloe had questions now.

"But why would they spread those kinds of lies. With everybody saying pretty much the same thing, it makes it look like its true."

"Good point." Sandra interjected not at all helping me in my defense. "I wondered the same thing myself."

"Listen, you guys, we have nothing to worry about." I tried to reassure them.

"We have plenty to worry about, Carl."

"Yeah, daddy, this is effecting all of our lives in a major way."

"The kids at school are all in our business, dad" they were all shooting at me and I didn't really have any definitive answers to give them that would make them feel any better.

"Just tell me one thing to ease my conscience. Were you or were you not having an inappropriate friendship with this guy, Patrick?" I appreciated Sandra wording her question that way, although our kids are smart and can read between lines.

"No. That man took things out of proportion then decided to try and publicize what he thought we had."

"What kind of business did you have with him, anyway?" She wasn't letting up.

"I was advising him on some relationship matters as well as his lifestyle choices."

"So you knew he was a homosexual?" Now in felt like I was being interrogated yet I answered anyway.

"Yes."

"And you were giving him advice dealing with his homosexual relationships?"

"Sandra, as a pastor, I'm responsible for drawing people to Christ no matter who they are or their sexual preference. I saw nothing wrong with that."

"Evidently, a lot of people found something wrong with that and have associated you with him. People's perceptions becomes reality which is hard to refute." I didn't say a word because she was right. From the outside looking in it would appear a certain way even if my intentions were pure.

"My fight now is to reverse this tailspin and protect you guys as best as possible. It's gonna be tough but I'm willing to try." I looked around at my family then to my wife before I spoke. "Will you guys forgive me for not bringing this to you sooner? I'm really gonna need your support on this." Chloe and Reecie gave me confirming nods. Sandra remained silent. I didn't expect anything less from her.

"Well, I have one more question, what do you think about Carl Jr. being a part of this family?" That question had all their mouths open. I hadn't made my mind up just yet but i wanted to throw it on the table since everything else was out there. "No need to answer right now, just think about it."

CHAPTER FIVE

Reecie

I WANTED TO SHOW DADDY WHAT ELSE I SAW ON SOME of those online tabloid sites, but I figured he had been through enough for the night. He and mom were at each other's throats. I've never seen her be so cold towards him before, in my eyes I thought they still loved each other. Maybe they do, its just not the kind of love I want to have.

My girls teased me a lot about this boy I have a crush on. I think he's digging on me too but I'm not quite sure. There's something about his swag that has me interested, the way he walks, the way he wears his clothes, and how he carries himself are attractive to me. I haven't been into boys much, they were always doing their thing and I was doing mine. Dancing and keeping my grades were tops in my book. Now that I'm in high school, the exposure has been greater as well as the selection.

"There goes Jalen, Sharice," Sasha teased using my real name instead of my nickname she always refers to me as. He was moving quickly to his locker like he was late for something.

"He just glanced over here to see his boo," she continued in tease mode.

"Who's his boo?" Joi asked playing along with Sasha's game.

"He knows Reecie is checking for him. The way she watches as he turns the combination on his lock. And the way he carries his tray in the lunch room."

"What about how he runs in the gym playing basketball?" Joi added.

"Yup, that too. Reecie is all into that Jalen pudding pop." I was completely blushed out from them.

"The only way he would known if I was checking for him is because of y'all two heffas always making a scene. He probably thinks I'm lame as hell for kicking it with y'all two."

"Oh don't act like you ain't drunk over him. Your eyes get dreamy whenever he's within twenty feet of you." Joi always had a way of over dramatizing the scene.

"I've seen you looking at him too, don't front girl" I snapped giving Sasha a high five.

"Shoot, I have to keep an eye on him to make sure he's suitable for you." She tried to save herself.

"Oh really?" I wasn't buying it but if that made her sleep better at night, more power to her.

"Yeah, Joi and I are like the neighborhood watch committee for bum dudes. If a bum steps this way, they gonna have a bad day." They gave each other a sista-girl fist pump.

"Y'all two are a mess. What we doing for lunch?" I asked.

"What you mean? We're doing the same thing we do everyday, taking our narrow asses to the cafeteria and eat them square pizzas."

"Ahh...excuse me, Reecie's the only one of us that don't have a narrow ass. You ain't seen all that she carrying around back there, Sash?" Joi peeked at my backside then gripped it in the middle of the hallway thoroughly embarrassing me. I jumped then slapped her hand away playfully.

"Damn, girl!"

"What? That's what Jalen's checking for. Might as well get used to some hands being on it." I wasn't comfortable talking about boys and sex stuff around my girls. I didn't know how experienced they were, I just knew how little I knew.

"Anyway, we can do something different today if y'all are game?" Both Sasha and Joi looked at each other then to me.

"What you talking about, Sharice? She said in her Arnold Drummond voice. Sasha stayed on YouTube watching old 80s sitcoms then quoting lines that nobody knew, those lines weren't even funny anymore.

"I know this girl, she's a Junior, she has open lunch which means she can go off school grounds to eat."

"So, what's that got to do with our young asses, we're only freshmen." Joi asked.

"We can go with her and eat some real food for a change. She just has to have us back by the start of 5th period." I hadn't given the plan much thought but the more I talked about it, the more I could see it happening.

"Girl, I don't know," Sasha whined. "How do you know this girl?"

"She's a friend of my sister Chloe."

"I thought your sister was a Senior over at Clover Hill?"

"She is. Elise transferred over here this year."

"Oh well, I don't have any money." Sasha stated.

"Yeah, me either. That's why I'm on this free lunch ticket," Joi said doing a dance.

"All I got is a twenty, if we eat light and y'all promise to get me back then I'll cover you today. I just want a change of scenery, besides it will be fun." I assured

I guess when they heard they wouldn't have to pay, that convinced them. When lunch period came, we eased out to the parking lot unnoticed. The girls and I climbed into Elise's Lexus, them in the backseat, me in the passenger. We were only riding a mile or so to a neighboring strip mall where a row of fast food restaurants were. My friends were quiet, not knowing what to say, I just made small talk with Elise. Honestly, I didn't really know her as well as I let on. She dropped Chloe off and I was out in the yard, my sister introduced us and that was pretty much it. At school, we spoke cordially out of respect.

Elise seemed nice and she did offer to let us ride with

her knowing she could get in a world of trouble, something just didn't add up with the whole thing. The Burger King drive through was crowded. After a few minutes we still hadn't moved an inch. She suggested we go inside and order rather than try to wait. It made sense because waiting would surely make us late and we didn't need that. Elise said she would swing around to get us.

As we went through the inside, Sasha and Joi looked at me suspiciously then asked. "She seems weird, do you trust her, Reecie?"

"She alright." I defended.

"I don't know, I just hope she comes back or we gonna be in some big trouble." Sasha said sounding scared.

We paid for our food and even had a chance to eat it before Elise showed up at the front of the Burger King parking lot. I spotted her first then went to the entrance. She beeped the horn for us to come out. I could see that my girls were agitated when we got in, Elise didn't say anything.

"Where did you go? We were ready after we ordered"

"I had to pick up a few things." Then she glared at me like who was I to question her. We pulled off and headed back to school.

The girls and I entered the same way we left without a trace. We went to our 5th period classes then met in the hallway afterwards. Nothing had been said about our disappearance. A few moments before 6th period we noticed a commotion around a row of lockers by the stairs. It was Elise, she was being questioned by two police officers. There was a small crowd that had to be pushed back by school authorities. One of the officers, a female began to search her person first, then her locker. Inside her locker was a bag with some items in it that still had price tags on them. They handcuffed her and pulled her away. As she walked by us she sneered.

"Bad luck bitches!"

What we didn't know was her little shoplifting escapades went on everyday at lunch hour. Up until that day she had never been caught. All I could think about was what if we were with her? The car she drove, the nice Lexus was being watched ever since things started coming up missing. We were being tailed back to school. They even saw her stop and pick us up at the Burger King. We were very fortunate the police didn't question us, it was Elise they were after. I'm sure glad too, I didn't know how I would explain that to my parents.

By the end of the day, I was in a down mood. When I met up with Sasha and Joi I could tell they were feeling the same way. I felt more of the burden for the close call, the quick and irrational decision to go with Elise could've gone way left. As I've heard my mom say on numerous occasions, by the grace of God we were spared. My girls still gave me a look of disdain.

"I'm sorry, y'all, I didn't know." I said before they even started in on me.

"What? And she didn't tell you she was a World Class Booster?" Joi joked which was a nice change to break the ill mood we were in.

"My grandmother always told me it's the quiet ones you have to watch, they sneaky! That girl was too quiet for my taste." Remarked Sasha.

"Well, I'm glad she didn't choose that time to start running her mouth and tell on us.

"I'm glad too, Reecie, for your sake. Me and Sasha would have had to make an example out of you if we went to jail." Joi kept a joke for every occasion. I ain't no punk and wasn't gonna be nobody's bitch either. I don't do the lesbo thang, girl." She slapped both of us dual high fives. We laughed hard until Jalen entered into our atmosphere again.

"On second thought, I could be his bitch," Joi blurted out flirtatiously. Sasha elbowed her in her side. "Oww! I'm just saying.

I didn't pay them any mind, Jalen and I made eye contact. I smiled which made him smile. He still had this coolness about him, it was as if he floated from his locker over in our direction. Our magnetism drew us closer. He was focused and I could tell he had something on his mind, me. There were a couple of girls trying to get his attention but he ignored them. He had his grown man stroll thing going on, feeling himself on the highest level. Then Bam! He bumped squarely into Mrs. Carmichael, the Art History teacher, knocking a pile of papers out of her hands. He was so embarrassed, he didn't even try to help her pick them up. I giggled as he tried miserably to regain his composure then he scurried off. My girls and I enjoyed that moment, probably because guys seem to do the stupidest things and we will somehow find something cute about it. I guess this was my introduction to how men will be from now until the end of time. My dad still does dumb stuff and now I see why my mom is so hard on him.

    I parted from my girls when my dad pulled up to the school. Some of the commotion had died down from then last time he came to pick me up. Sure the Internet was still buzzing with the rumors about the "Problem Pastor" but high school kids don't stay on things too long. Social media can make news old quick.

    "Hey baby girl!" He greeted me with the joy of a proud father. "What you know good?" He asked trying to sound hip. I chuckled at his attempt.

    "Just regular school stuff. Nothing major." I'm glad I didn't have to report what could've been a catastrophe today. Since it went in my favor, what he didn't know wouldn't hurt him.

    "That's good. You know you can share anything with me, Sharice. I want to keep things up front and honest with the family."

    "I hear you, dad."

    "Good. You and your sister mean the world to me. I try my best to shield you from harm, that's why it bothers me so to see you guys effected by the things going on with me. It wasn't my intention for everything to be so public."

    "Its ok, dad. You say Chloe and I mean the world to you, what about mom?" There was a pause and I knew it wasn't because he was concentrating on the road.

    "I can't lie, your mom and I have hit a rough patch.

Our love for each other has dwindled. Right now, we're channeling what we have left in us through to you guys. As adults we have to see what's most important and that's our children. Even though I preach that marriage is an institution that should remain forever, the reality is some good things come to an end."

"So you're saying you and mom are over?" Tears starting to well up hoping I wasn't about to hear the worst.

"No, I'm not saying that at all. We're just going through a transition and its just gonna take some work. Its not how I want it to be but it is what it is." I laughed at his use of that saying. It was actually appropriate.

"You think you're cool don't you, dad?" I picked at him causing him to crack a smile.

"Cooler than the other side of the pillow!" He said cracking himself up. "You don't know anything about that. The late, great Stuart Scott made that phrase famous."

"Who?" I was lost.

"He was a sportscaster that died from a terminal cancer well before his time. But he lived life all the way until his last breath."

"Oh, that's really sad, dad."

"What made him so great was the victory he had proclaimed. You could tell it wasn't him speaking but God using him in those last moments to get a message out. I wish I had that kind of strength in my weakest moments."

"I believe you do, dad, you just don't know it."

CHAPTER SIX

Adrian

COOKIE AND I WERE HAVING A GREAT CONVERSATION. We had been on the phone the better part of two hours. Just when we were about to hit another subject, she hung up the line abruptly. I knew exactly what was going on, I just didn't want to accept it. That wasn't the first time she had to end a call with me due to her husband showing up. To be totally honest, the whole situation was getting frustrating. The way we talked and the closer we were becoming, it almost seemed like her husband, Carl, was knocking my groove like a third wheel. It may sound crazy but he seemed more like an intruder than the other way around.

Dave Hollister had a song saying "if you take care of home, you don't have to worry about your girl" that song was made for this situation. The truth is the truth, if a woman isn't happy at home she will find happiness elsewhere. If she is willing to entertain outside attention, then the foundation is not as stable as it once was.

Cookie, at first, used me as a sounding board for her problems. As a married woman and the First Lady she found it hard to find someone to confide in. Everyone around her was so judgmental, the church expected her to live by a certain standard. It didn't dawn on them that everyone under that church roof was a human being having feelings and emotions. If they thought they were exempt from the problems of daily life, they were living a lie.

A lot of her church family are living lies. She would tell me about older ladies, the ones who wore the huge showy hats on Sunday, who would give you advice about life meanwhile their lives were less than desirable. Like a lady named Ms. Agnes for example. She told me Ms. Agnes was always trying to tell the other members how the should conduct themselves. When you talk about church gossip, she was the queen of it. For years, Sister Agnes, as she preferred to be called, would keep tabs on everyone's business by floating from Deacon to Deacon, then parishioners, then ushers, prying and pressing for information.

She was the one who would be at the Bible study on Wednesdays, Friday night service, Saturday afternoon bake sales where she furnished all the pies and cakes, then right back early Sunday morning catching Sunday school service and all the services for the day. To the outside, untrained eye, Sister Agnes appeared to be everybody's favorite Auntie or Grandmother who loved her church. In actuality, it was a cover up for a bigger picture she didn't expect everyone to see.

Cookie said it was later discovered that Sister Agnes Calloway had something deeper going on in her world. Agnes' late husband Luther, was a truck driver, a very successful one, in fact he owned a fleet of eighteen wheelers that he commissioned out to make runs all over the country. All you had to have was a CDL and an up to standard insurance and you could bring in a paycheck based on the contract. Luther, after he became too old to drive himself, would work on pulling in contracts for his drivers. That was working well for a couple of years until he became ill. He eventually passed away and left the business fledgling.

Agnes thought she could pick up where Luther left off. She tried for a season or so to keep up the pace but the results just weren't the same. Soon the drivers started to fall off, leaving her with a bunch of trucks and bills that needed to be paid. There was one driver that decided to stick around and approached Agnes with a plan. She wasn't sure she had it in her but thought about it then took a chance.

Elijah, or Eli, wasn't just the average driver, he was a hustler. He was the man that Agnes needed to run her show. He was young, aggressive, and most importantly hungry for the money. He told Mama Agnes that he could provide her with a crew of certified drivers, all with a special set of skills, networking , as he referred to it. She didn't ask too many questions about what he proposed, it was a blessing that she had someone to help her with the business. It was what she prayed for, Luther would want it that way.

It didn't take long before the plan went into motion and the money started to roll in. It was, however, the route in which it was coming in that was in question. Eli organized his team and equipped them with plenty of product to be transported and distributed throughout the country. The product happened to be illegal drugs. They were packaged like parcels and loaded fully into these eighteen wheelers then delivered to customers. It was the new wave to move narcotics undetected, it even went undetected to Agnes.

Two years into operations and the money was beginning to draw the attention of not just the D.E.A. but also the IRS. It was hard to account for the amount of income the upstart trucking company was accruing. As always, all good things come to an end. One of Eli's drivers got sloppy with the paperwork by not providing the proper invoices that was legitimizing the deliveries on his routes. Actually, he was skimming money and didn't want to leave a paper trail. That greedy move proved to be costly for everyone and put Ms. Agnes in some serious hot water.

Drug enforcement agents conducted a large scale investigation on the company in conjunction with the IRS. If one didn't get them, the other would. A sting operation was set up to catch the big fish. Eli's cross country trip fell right into their net. He was captured in New Mexico after being under surveillance making drops at various locations along the way. He was arrested on the spot, trucks and cargo confiscated and turned in as evidence by the authorities.

They squeezed information from Elijah forcing him to dime out the lady he called Mama Agnes. The arrest came shortly after by local agents. Agnes Calloway, age 74, was detained and questioned about operating an interstate drug trafficking organization. The lawyer she quickly hired eloquently negotiated some lengthy probation as opposed to prison, which she couldn't do due to her age. That, and her obvious lack of knowledge that the operation was actually going on. She adamantly explained that she was being taken advantage of and the DA showed leniency. Money that she put away from initial runs that weren't accounted for was used for her legal services; money well spent.

Her church family was clueless to her past activities. If the truth came out, her reputation as the wholesome matriarch would be tarnished indeed. When she felt comfortable enough to be herself without her secret being revealed, she returned to her meddling ways. It wasn't until a surprised guest showed up at a newcomer's Sunday service and proudly introduced himself as Agnes Calloway's interstate drug runner. This public announcement, coming from one Elijah Oliver who made bond on one of his charges, drew 'oohs' and 'ahhs' in the crowded congregation. All eyes were on Ms. Agnes who for the first time was speechless. She quietly excused herself from the sanctuary and the church altogether never to be seen again.

Cookie vowed to me that she didn't want to be that

woman, living a lie among her church family. Yet here she was living a complicated life, full of disappointments and lost hope. In the beginning our talks were about her quest for long lasting happiness, something she thought was possible in a marriage with Carl. The more we spoke the more she mentioned the feeling of being trapped. Listening to Cookie detail her life, it appeared like she was in a prison in her own world.

Carl had made it hard for her to leave even if she wanted to. Their home, he owned it. The phone that she and the kids use, were on his plan, which meant he had unlimited access to pull up messages, pictures, even call logs. She never really felt like she had any privacy. Even her car was in his name. As the Pastor of the church, he was the primary provider so it made it easier to have all the bills centrally controlled by him. Psychologically, that would make anyone feel imprisoned.

Talking to me, she said, was an escape from her reality. Where I thought she was helping me, I was actually a help mate to her. I never could imagine my prison world be an escape to someone who was living free. In her eyes, she didn't see herself as living free. With all the responsibility of being a First Lady at the church, then having to come home to that environment, it made her feel like the walls of her life were closing in on her.

Cookie asked me how do I cope with the time. I told her I take it one day at a time. Whether we're on the inside or out, that's all we can do. She felt comfort in hearing that from me. I realized at that moment that women don't require much. Of course, there are those who chase men for whatever material items they can get but they fall into their own category. I'm speaking of those women who value simplicity. Compliments and support are the things they hold onto. As a woman who had been through a lot in life, Cookie deserved more.

I felt helpless. A man always thinks he can throw on a cape, swoop down and save the day. Protect, provide, comfort, support, these are just some of the many qualities that make up a good man. Over the years, I've sat on my bunk, the thin piece of mattress laying over a steel frame, taking time to reflect. I really took inventory of my past then thought about what kind of man I wanted to be. How would a woman accept me? At this stage in my life, after serving time, what perception would women have of me? Pam and I spoke about this once, she said because there are so many men locked up, women formulate their own views. She's heard women in the world think that men who have done more than seven years in prison are subject to be gay. Even though that's a gross generalization, it's their view and they're entitled to it.

Was this what I had to look forward to upon my release? I hear all sorts of stories like the men, who actually are gay, come out and go back to being straight, get with women who are naive, then spread whatever disease they're carrying. Its sad, but I've seen guys who were openly gay in here, go to the visitation room to see their girlfriends from the street, kiss and hug on them the whole visit, then go back to their dorm afterwards and be with his dude.

I've heard the world was just as sick. Where its OK for a man to dress up like a woman, take hormones to get a body like a woman, talk like a woman, all to trick a man into thinking he's a woman. From the stories I've heard, homosexuality has no boundaries. For a man that wants a second chance and a fresh start, its scary. One of the main reasons I'm trying to build strong relationships now. Cookie has shown me that she is real and I can deal with that. I just can't deal with her being someone else's wife.

CHAPTER SEVEN

Cookie

"Why am I finding it hard to believe him?" I asked Maxine. I dropped by her office hoping she would be free to talk. I knew I was taking a chance, Max stayed busy with appointments and I didn't schedule one for today. The friendship card comes in handy every now and then.

"Cookie, you don't think there's a chance he's telling the truth? The way you said he came in and addressed you and the girls shows that he had good intentions." I just rolled my eyes at her. "Please don't tell me you did that when he was confessing to you." I smiled knowing what I did.

"Max, I was there listening to him, and I was there at the restaurant also. I saw Carl and that guy, Patrick having an animated discussion. This man was obviously determined to get his point across and didn't care who heard."

"And you really feel like Patrick is gay?" She asked as if I had no clue on the subject.

"Maxine Stinson, I know the difference between a straight and a gay man. That man was definitely gay, besides Carl admitted that he was giving him relationship and lifestyle advice at the church. My feelings are that there were other meetings outside his church office. For someone to get that attached to you just from a few random counseling sessions, it all seems kind of odd."

"I don't know Cookie, we've had a number sessions of our own and you're starting to look appealing to me. Maybe we should become an item." My eyes nearly bucked out of my head until I realized she was playing with me.

"Girl, you're crazy!" I playfully pushed her. "All I'm saying is its not a good look. Not for him, not for our family, and especially not for the ministry."

"How's the church reacting to all these allegations? I know they're tripping. Church gossip is probably at an all time high."

"I'm not quite sure, I haven't been as active as I used to be." I confessed.

"Don't tell me you're losing your faith?"

"No, never that. My faith is in God, nothing will ever change that. If I'm losing anything, its my motivation to be around those people. Its one thing to have to be around Carl at home but at the church where he performs in front of the congregation, it all seems so fake to me. And lately the attendance has fallen off so that shows me just how loyal they are to their Pastor." She looked at me incredulously.

"I have to ask you this, Cookie."

"What?"

"What kind of public support are you showing? I mean regardless of what's going on at home, as the First Lady of the church your role is to stand by his side, especially in the dark times. How do you think he feels? His staff and congregation could abandon him, but not his wife."

"Whose side are you on, Max?" I cried out.

"I'm on the side of logic. I just wanted you to see it from his side. I'm not discrediting anything you're saying or questioning your reasons from pulling back from going to church. It just sounded to me that your reasons were selfish, and in a marriage, the team comes first." Damn if it didn't sound like Max was turning on me.

"Maybe I am being selfish in my thinking. I've been a team player for so long and it wasn't getting me any wins, just a spank on the butt and a 'nice game'."

"Well, I see someone is getting their inner SportsCenter on."

"Whatever. Bottom line is he's getting on my nerves, girl. Can we talk about something else?"

"Sure, what's on your mind?" She was happy to switch gears.

"Remember when we were on the phone and I asked you about those guys you were hooked up with, the ones with the black SUV?"

"Yeah, what about them?" She asked casually asked, obviously not knowing how serious the situation is.

I went on to tell her how they were in my neighborhood, then how they were in my driveway looking at my car. I even told her how terrified I was when one of them locked eyes with me when I was peeking through the blinds. When they left I was relieved but was still unsure of what they wanted or what their next move would be.

"Cookie, I didn't know. Why would they be stalking you when they had a problem with me?"

"Maybe they know I'm helping you." I lied knowing all too well why they were after me. My guess was one of them were still in that house when me and Gabriel sped off. I was so concerned about the money and Gabriel's leg, I didn't consider who may have witnessed us leaving. I hadn't told Maxine what had happened, not quite sure if I was going to.

"I don't see how, unless they saw you the day I went to court. Maybe they've been following you from here. We could be all day trying to figure out their logic.

"Speaking of court, you have a date coming up, don't you?"

"Don't remind me."

"What's your lawyer saying?"

"Not much. That's the thing, you'd think she would have some sound advice for me. All she is saying is hopefully the judge will take into consideration the evidence about me being under duress, the fear of threats by those goons caused me to perjure myself."

"That's what's she's going with? That's not solid at all."

"I know. Its a long shot. Putting my hopes in a judge that has already found me guilty of the offense once, is not something I feel confident with."

I don't blame her for the way she's feeling. Her lawyer should have a better strategy than that, there has to be some sort of way to prove that she was in fact under duress. If Max doesn't go in front of the judge with some evidence, something concrete, she will be doomed for sure. The only thing I can think of is having one of those goons admit that he paid her to change her statement. Now what would be the chances of them openly admitting that, unless they get caught on tape saying it.

I still fulfilled my monthly obligation, driving down to Lofton State Prison for our prison ministry. For one, I believe in keeping my dedication to service of those seeking God's word. Those guys had a certain longing to hear the Lord speak and the spirit always flows in that place. Of course, I'm anxious to see Adrian too. Ever since he hit me with the news about him coming home, I've had some restless nights. Part of me has been giddy all over. What would life be like with him here with me? If our conversation and attraction was this strong now, I can imagine how close we would get in person. The other part of me is worried about what to do about Carl.

I can tell that we're drifting apart emotionally. I don't even like sleeping in the same room with him. At times, I'll get up in the middle of the night and climb into bed with Reecie. She'll stir a little bit but she welcomes me. My body yearns for affection and I don't feel attracted to Carl. I know it sounds cruel to say that about a husband you've been with for almost 17 years but when those years haven't been blissful, eventually change will come.

Adrian has been the fresh air of change that has blown in. What I've missed emotionally, he has filled effortlessly. It didn't come with a bunch of meaningless game or sexual innuendos, it came in the form of compassion, understanding, and a little harmless flirting. In fact, the flirting went both ways with each party treading lightly, him more out of respect. He was very gentleman-like, allowing me to take the lead. There was an unspoken understanding that I had way more to lose than he did and he was aware of that.

With our friendship being pressure free, it let me figure things out at home at my pace. Besides, there was an uncertainty about when we would actually be together, until he dropped the bomb on me the other day. Now my mind was racing. The anticipation, the possibilities, the anxiety, even the fantasies all were within reach and to be honest I don't know how I'm going to handle it.

I remember mornings after a sleepless night with Adrian on my mind. I made the fatal mistake of trying make love to Carl using Adrian as my motivation. His name crept out of my mouth and I'm almost sure Carl heard it. I know that was wrong but I couldn't help what I was feeling at the time. In the heat of passion I lost all control of my faculties, thoughts, and worst of all my tongue. So I saved my fantasies for the shower.

With the shower running hot, I took the adjustable head, with the multiple functions, and gave myself a much needed massage. I imagined it was Adrian's strong hands moving rhythmically all over my body. For my age I still had my curves, nice firm breasts with large brown nipples that hardened at the slightest touch. My booty was round and soft, holding its shape well, a nice gripping was in the cards. With my eyes closed, I pictured him rubbing my shoulders then soaping me up and down with my body scrub.

In my mind, his hands were magical, touching me, making my skin tingle. Soft moans emitted from my mouth when he palmed my breast, squeezing them with just the right amount of pressure to make my nipples arouse. Not being able to resist, Adrian ran his tongue across their taut texture driving me wild. The more pleasure he saw me receiving, the more intense he made his tongue dance. Over and over, he fluttered the tip then kissed with full lips like a baby savoring their first nursing. I was in ecstasy and didn't want him to stop.

I wanted him to go further. Pushing his head southward, I directed his path to what I desired, something I haven't experienced in ages. I held onto his head and placed it between my legs, an area that had been void of attention longer than I plan to mention. Without a second thought, he reached around and gripped my ass pulling me into his waiting lips. My light bush down there hadn't been shaved this month but Adrian didn't seem to mind and it definitely didn't impede his progress.

He gently parted my throbbing lips with two fingers, leading in with his soft lips and elongated tongue. He forced himself inside, sucking, licking, and kissing his way to my pleasure point. Adrian was hitting spots I didn't even know I had. My moans became shrills and screams, giving way to his masterful oral lovemaking. I could only imagine what the rest of his skill set were like if this was how he made an introduction.

When he curled his tongue's tip underneath my clit, touching that big girl spot, I nearly lost all control, grabbing a firm hold of his head. I held it there until I released all of the pent up emotion that head been trapped inside for years. Shaking uncontrollably, I thanked him over and over and over again.

"Oh thank you. Thank you. Thank you!" I whispered out a bit more audibly than I thought.

"Sister Andrews, are you alright?" The voice sounded vaguely familiar. I opened my eyes and it took me a moment to focus on my surroundings. Oh my God! We're on the van, with the worship team. I can't believe what just happened.

"Ah....Sister Allen, I'm good." She gave me a sly grin then announced that we were almost at the prison.

"You may want to get yourself together before we go in. Oh and don't worry, no one else heard you." She smiled. "Those dreams are something, huh?" I was thoroughly embarrassed now. She knew. I'm just glad it was her, Sister Allen was my girl. "I'm sure you will find it nice to known that the men up front are clueless. Otherwise, they may have had a tough time giving the message," she joked.

"I'm sorry."

"No need to apologize. I've been there, maybe not on the church van, but hey, you never know where your dreams take you."

"Your right, that sure was a wonderful trip, one that I didn't need a van to travel"

"Well welcome back. Oh and there's something I need to inform you about your husband. I'll tell you on the way back. We're at the facility."

CHAPTER EIGHT

The Watchers

"THINGS JUST AIN'T THE SAME FOR GANGSTERS!" Rico blurted out to no one in particular. "We don't get the respect like we used to." He continued hoping to get a reaction.

"Man, what the hell are you talking about? You ain't no gangsta, Rico." The man snorted without even looking up. He had his mini assault rifle dismantled on the table while he cleaned each piece individually.

Demani was always on Rico's case. He was one of the elders of the crew and with Rico being the last member added, it was his responsibility to keep him in line. Pappo, was the undisputed leader of their unit, he didn't like to refer to themselves as a crew or a gang, those connotations drew unnecessary heat. Although, they did have affiliations, Pappo, preferred to operate under his own agenda. His main agenda was clear, free his nephew, Richie Rich Crawford.

Their appeal process took a crash when their ace in the hole, testimony from Maxine Stimson, was viewed as not satisfactory. The judge considered it contradictory to her original statement and didn't hesitate to cite her for perjury. That was the absolute worst scenario they could hear. Pappo, Demani, and Ricardo, Rich's cousins, all sat in the back of the courtroom totally astonished at the outcome. Pappo paid good money, $50,000 worth, to get her to cooperate with them. All she had to do was rewrite her statement to one more favorable to their side. Now they had to come up with another option, something they were running out of.

Demani Crawford was devastated when his first cousin, Rich got caught up and was locked up. Growing up they were as thick as thieves, literally. Together, they would do little petty crimes like a couple of car theft/joyrides, then they graduated to B&E's where they would split their profits. As they got older their interests changed. Demani moved to robbing while Richie decided to venture into the drug trade.

Rich's rise to fame came faster than Demani's and he couldn't have been happier. In fact, Demani was the one who gave him the moniker, Richie Rich, named after the super wealthy cartoon kid. Demani's operation was more hit or miss while Richie's income steadily increased. It was the crew of guys that surrounded Demani who created a level of greed and envy that infected Demani's usually cool demeanor. Rich wasn't what you would call a showy or boastful man but he was extremely proud of his success in the drug business. For his first time, he was very proud of his decision to hustle.

With Demani and his robbing crew nickel and diming it to low level notoriety, Richie Rich's Forever Rich gang were known all around the DMV. That's saying a lot because the D.C., Maryland, and Virginia has been considered a drug lord's hub dating back to the 80's. No matter how close Demani and Rich claimed to be, it was hard to dismiss a natural jealousy between men. Family was one thing but a man's ego would cause a man to question even his own flesh and blood.

Unbeknownst to Demani, his crew devised a plan to rob his cousin, Richie Rich. They were angered by their leader's nonchalant attitude towards Richie's flamboyant rise to stardom. Rich never considered his cousin a threat, it was unwritten that family never rides on family, so he kept his eyes elsewhere for enemies. This was just what Demani's crew was banking on, him being totally oblivious to their scheme. If there was anyone Richie didn't have to worry about was a threat coming from his cousin, Demani.

On a night where business was routine for Rich, he decided to stop in on one of his most successful drug spots. This particular house he purchased had become his most lucrative operation. He had no worries about their productivity. As a boss, it was always favorable to keep watch over the ins and outs of his business.

In business, timing was everything, and for Rich his timing wasn't the best on that fateful night. As traffic flowed around the house with money flowing, all of a sudden a bevy of cars and vans came to a screeching halt out front. Out jumped armed masked assailants, dressed in hoodies and fatigues. Rich and his men didn't hesitate to initiate shooting. Fire exploded out of the automatic weapons as people ran and ducked for cover.

Rich, himself, found a safe distance to cover himself while the shooting continued. Watching from a far, he noticed one of the cars looked vaguely familiar, it was one of the flashy rides that had been to the house before, one of Demani's people. An exchange of gun fire insued with Rich aiming his sights on one particular man. He aimed for his target, as did another one of Rich's men. Two shots rang out just as a barrage of police cars came flying in. A bullet connected taking down one of the hooded men. To his surprise the shot he fired didn't leave his weapon.

"Freeze! Get on the ground now!" The uniformed officer shouted at Rich. He was cuffed and carted off in a patrol car. On his way, he couldn't help to think how his cousin Demani had set him up, sending him to jail in the process. The man he aimed at was the lucky one, his gun jamming saved his life. There was a woman across who watched the events like her favorite television show. She and Rich connected eyes as he was taken away.

To make matters worse, Rich's main money man, who later got arrested at the scene, gave testimony on the witness stand against Rich, naming him as the shooter, causing the death of Robert Mitchell. He knew that he didn't do it, his gun never fired. To his unbelief, he couldn't understand someone who had been so loyal basically pointed the finger at his mentor. What also amazed Rich was Demani's presence in the courtroom. He pleaded to Rich with his eyes that he didn't set him up. Looking back at him, he even saw him mouth he word "it wasn't me". Rich just turned around disregarding the gesture, focusing on his future, hoping for the best.

Demani sent countless letters to Rich while he has been at Lofton State Prison facility, all have been unanswered. It took for Pappo to overhear a heated argument between Demani and one of his men about the failed robbery attempt of Rich's spot. Demani was furious with him because he gave specific instructions not to hit Rich, he was family. They went against the code, which had consequences. Pappo and his dear nephew had a heart to heart discussion where he vowed to make Rich understand.

First on Pappo's agenda was to get a handle on the Maxine Stinson situation. She was now out on bond and has returned back to her counseling practice. It has also been rumored that she has befriended a woman they have identified as Sandra Andrews. Through his research, they found out she's the First Lady at the Victory in Faith Baptist Church. One way or another he was going to get to her.

He had other reasons for targeting her, by attaching herself to Maxine Stimson, this Sandra Andrews has just put herself on the hit list. What she didn't realize was that one of his good men got killed and another wounded after her and that young kid got away with some money of his. Pappo recruited his youngest nephew, Ricardo, also known as Rico to keep fresh eyes on Mrs. Andrews and her family. Pappo has learned a lot about patience, when he was ready to pounce he'd give the word. Once he and his boys visited the neighborhood of this Andrews woman, took pictures of her vehicle, and gathered more info on her, then he would make his move. Her time would come.

CHAPTER NINE

Carl

Now let me see what she has going on with this phone. I'm glad I have all of their accounts tied in to my laptop. Chloe and Reecie get a little leeway because they are kids and haven't caused me to be suspicious but Sandra, she has been acting really strange lately. Something was going on between her and this Adrian fellow, I just had to find out what.

Her sudden desire not to want to sleep in our bed told that things were changing. Our lack of intimacy was another sign that our marriage was going south. I still wasn't willing to accept the fact that she didn't love me anymore. I've counseled plenty of married couples and listened to each party give me a laundry list of issues they say are reasons to separate. I do my best to find the positives and focus on those. My main goal was to keep couples together. Now, here I am in the same boat, rowing upstream. Who was in position to counsel me? Sandra on many occasions has mentioned going to counseling, I turned her down every time.

Unlike her counselor, this Maxine Stinson woman, if I were to consider counseling, I prefer it come from the church. There's just something about a total stranger being all in our business. Sandra may like doing that but I don't particularly care to engage with outsiders. Now, with the church, that's supposed to be a bit more unbiased. The covering of God is the equalizer and I'd much rather have the Almighty as a referee between relationship matters than a stranger.

So instead of us working it out, we have these unresolved issues in our home. Which leads me to believe there's something serious going on outside of our marriage. When behavioral patterns change, the one closest to you is the first one to notice. In my case, I'd be remiss if I didn't see a change in Sandra and I think whatever's she's hiding is in this phone.

While she was at work I have ample opportunity to peruse the call logs. From the records, there was definitely evidence that she has been conversing with her therapist even after working hours. This leads me to believe that their relationship is deeper than what she leads on. I'm sure she's confiding in her, divulging all sorts of negative things about our family, especially me.

What I found interesting was the frequent calls to and from a "301" prefix. I pretty much know Sandra's friends from around here and they have the new "240" prefix. Plus this 301 number was new activity. I wondered if this was this Adrian guy. There's one way to find out.

A twinge of guilt came over me while I dialed the number but I proceeded with the mission. The phone rang four times before a male voice answered.

"Who this?" The voice was deep so I wasn't sure if it was him.

"Is this Adrian?" I asked cautiously not knowing what to expect.

"Who's asking?" Again this person questioned obviously annoyed at the disturbance. I didn't know I should volunteer my identity, it may had not been his number. I took a chance.

"My name is Pastor Carlton Andrews."

"OK, so how can I help you?"

"First of all, I need to know if this is Adrian?"

"Yes, speaking."

"Your number showed up on my wife's phone."

"And your wife is?" Now this guy wants to play dumb, I wasn't in the mood for games.

"Look, young man, I know all about you." I lied trying to sound tough. "I know you and my wife have been talking real regularly."

"And how is it that you know this?"

"I have my ways"

"You must be spying, what are you a secret agent?" He must think this is a game.

"I don't have to spy, when she is my wife. Her business is my business. Now let me tell you what I've put together. You know my church comes to your facility once a month, that means I know that you're an inmate. I was in service that night when you and MY wife were exchanging flirtatious glances." He was quiet which tells me that what I as saying had some truth to it.

"My question to you is why haven't you confronted Cookie about these discoveries?" Cookie? He refers to her by her nickname? Wow.

"Oh I intend to, but right now I'm confronting you, man to man. Well, actually I feel like I'm the only man in this situation because a real man doesn't mess with another man's wife."

"For one, Cookie and are just friends. Unless you have a problem with her having male friends, you are the one with a problem. You maybe one of those controlling types who don't allow their wife to have male friends. That sounds like an insecurity." He shot back defending his position.

"From what I see, you two are more than friends."

"What exactly do you see, Pastor?"

I wanted to tell him how Sandra looks when he calls. I wants to tell him how different she's been acting ever since she and the ministry comes back from the prison. I wanted to express to him that I sense her drifting further apart as a result of their interaction. There were so many things I wanted to tell him but couldn't bring myself to do it.

"I see enough." I said deflated. "If I were you, I'd be careful."

"And if I were you, I'd be having a beautiful life with my beautiful wife, problem free." He threw a hard punch to my gut, below the belt. I kept my cool not trying to engage in a verbal battle with him.

"I'll be in touch." I left him with that as I decided how I was going to handle the situation. I may need to watch them a little more closely.

❦

The church had some repairs that needed to be tended to, not to mention the landscaping had been neglected for months. The overall appearance of our facility was being diminished by not finding qualified people to service us. Although the inner decor had anyone thinking we were doing well, it was merely a facade, masking the real problems. Its amazing how this church mirrored my life.

Deacon Reynolds handed me a list of potential contractors so I started making some calls. Seemed like the contractors I talked to had either a little bit of this or missing a whole lot of that. Noting was right for what we needed. I was operating under limited budget and simply wasn't willing to pay an arm and a leg for labor, I could get a mom and pop operation to handle some plumbing issues and a little grass cutting.

I thought for a moment then a brilliant revelation came to me, maybe I should give my son a try. He said he was good with his hands, I could show him a minor project and see if he has skills. He could be good or he could be a bust which will end up costing me anyway. If he has my genes I'm banking on him being able to get the job done.

"What's up, Pop?" He answered the phone on he first ring. I still haven't gotten used to him calling me Pop yet.

"I want you to stop by the church, there's some things around here that need to be tightened up and I believe you're just the man for the job."

"Really? You have some work for me?" He asked excitedly

"Yup, sure do. Just come in and see Deacon Reynolds, he's over our labor department."

"Great! I sure will. Thanks, dad, you won't regret this."

"You're welcome. Do a good job and I'll have some more work for you."

"I got you"

Sister Allen usually allocates the funds for our contractors and any maintenance fees. Today I'll alert her that we'll be saving some money by using another source.

"Pastor, I have a call for you. He says its urgent that he speak with you personally." My assistant said peeking her head into my office.

"Patch it through."

"Carl?" He asked in a low tone. "This is Patrick." I was in shock to hear his voice. After all the commotion and embarrassment he caused, not to mention the ridicule I've experienced over the past month, he had some nerve calling here. I really thought that chapter was closed, he was still hovering over me like a black cloud.

"What is it?" I made sure he heard the short tone.

"I know things ended sourly for us and I caused you a lot of stress."

Patrick had no idea how my life has changed since he entered into it. What started out as a platonic counseling session turned it into a situation where this man developed a delusional relationship. At first he came to the church as a man seeking advice. He came in alone saying his partner was too ashamed to come to church and discuss their problems. So all of our conversations were coming from a one sided perception.

There were times when he asked to meet at a restaurant, I would tell Sandra I was working late just to clear time to counsel with him. I felt like his issues were sensitive and in need of my time. He explained how his partner was having mixed feelings about their future. They had made plans to marry but the realization of what was to come frightened him. Same sex marriages weren't as readily accepted in the Northern states as they were in the Midwest or the more liberal West coast. Patrick's emotions were thrown amiss as if tossed into a blender with no top on it. My main concern was to keep him from doing anything drastic. His partner didn't want any part of the public outcry and decided to end things before it got out that he was participating in a gay union.

Patrick insisted on continued counseling and I agreed thinking his psyche was fragile. I knew from past experience that situations like this could turn suicidal and no one wants blood on their hands. As a Pastor, a minister of God has the responsibility of bringing people closer to the Almighty. People are people, no matter their gender or sexual preference. I figured I was doing the will of God by not showing prejudice, little did I know it would come back to bite me.

After so many meetings, Patrick began to change in his demeanor as well as his way of thinking. No longer was he focusing on fighting to keep his relationship together with his partner, he started inquiring about meeting privately, he even suggested coming to my home, which I quickly negated. I regretted him having my cell number because he called at all kinds of inconvenient times, making it appear secretive. The whole thing was awkward and unprofessional.

So to the outside eyes, it would seem like we were having some sort of dealings. When I look back, the more I tried to help Patrick, the worst things were looking for me. It was my reputation on the line if the perception of what it looked like got out. My credibility was going to be questioned not his; I had way more to lose yet I still tried to end it amicably. All for what? To be exposed to social media as this person hiding secrets. He doesn't have a clue as to how hard its going to be to gain the trust of my peers, my congregation, and most of all my family. Maybe he doesn't care at all.

"Patrick, there was never any us." I said as calmly as I could, hoping not to raise his emotional level. "And yes, you made life for me very difficult, I hope you realize that." There was an eerie silence which told me he was processing what I said.

"What do you mean there was no us? Sure there was. We were moving towards something special. How could you not see that?"

"Patrick, all I've been trying to do is help you. I'm a married man with a family and you know that."

"What about when you said if your wife wanted to separate, you'd take her up on it?" He caught me off guard with that one.

"Yes I did say that, but I was merely letting you know that when couples go through issues you do have options." I tried to recover.

"I thought I may have been an option for you," he sounded dejected.

"No Patrick. And I'm sorry if I made you feel otherwise. Now I have to pick up the broken pieces of my life."

"I guess we're not too much different after all" then he abruptly hung up the phone, leaving me to wonder what his next move was going to be.

Deacon Reynolds came in frantically without knocking. "Hey, Deacon, is there something wrong?"

"Did my son come meet with you about the work?" He had a sullen look on his face.

"Ahh...yes, Pastor. I got him situated then started him on that small project in the Reserve Room."

"That's right, the leaking pipe in the bathroom, how did he do? He said he was good with his hands," I said raving like a proud poppa.

"Well, Sir, its hard for me to report this but we didn't secure the room before he got started and because he wasn't the normal contractor nobody noticed him in the bathroom. He must've had the door closed when Sister Aikens brought in the offerings for the weekly drop." I had a sinking feeling in my gut however I heard him out. "Now you know, usually we let the drop get secured before anyone enters the room but the place was empty and no one thought to check the bathroom. Sister Aiken left the satchel on the table then went to go find Sister Allen so she could do her accounting thing. By the time she came back both the satchel and your son were gone.

I was in shock. There was no way that this was happening. I had just been robbed by my own son, the person I asked to come in. The money, God's money, was not the issue, anyone who had the audacity to steal from a church deserved whatever consequences that came with it. What I couldn't understand was why it had to be my son, and why me? I quickly tried the number he left me. It was the only one I had for him, so it was worth a shot.

"The number you have dialed has been changed or disconnected," the recording answered just as I figured.

CHAPTER TEN

Reecie

CHLOE AND I HAVEN'T BEEN THE BEST EXAMPLE OF BIG sister/little sister combination in the world, but she's all I have. Lately she has been distant around the house spending most of her time on her phone with Gabriel, her on again-off again boyfriend. Their relationship was strange and I could always tell when things were going well. When they were good, Chloe was good, when they were on the outs, she was someone you didn't want to be around.

Today I had some more questions about boys and I'd much rather get advice from her than from mom, or the girls at school. Mom would just give me the old fashion version of what I need, my girls don't really know enough so they recycle something they've heard elsewhere which is no earthly good to me. Plus they could be haters at times. They would tell you something wrong hoping things don't work out; sabotage was their middle name when they saw something they wanted. That's why I'm always skeptical of their advice for me concerning Jalen, especially Joi. I know deep down she wants him for herself, but he's showing an obvious interest in me. Her true colors will reveal itself sooner or later.

"Chloe, I didn't know your girl, Elise was a major league shoplifter." She just chuckled knowingly.

"Oh she's at it again? She called herself retiring after her last brush with the law."

"You mean she's got a history of doing that?" I wish I would've known, although I never knew a quick trip to a fast food spot would turn into an excuse to boost.

"Yeah, she's always had sticky fingers, that's the reason she had to transfer from my school to yours. The school security caught her attempting to steal some school paraphernalia from our school store. Instead of pressing charges, they allowed her the opportunity to leave, giving her a second chance."

"Well, her chances are about up. The real cops took her away the other day for shoplifting in a local strip mall." I purposely omitted the part that put us with her.

"I thought she was alright, you know, cool?"

"She is, just not the one to be rolling with." Gee, thanks for the warning, I thought.

"I see. Anyway, can I ask you something?"

"Shoot," she said now focusing her attention back on her phone.

"Its about a boy." I confessed which caused her to pause for a second then smile.

"Ahh....boys, its about time, Reecie. This is around them age you're supposed to be curious."

"There's this boy at school that I like."

"Is he cute?" She asked making me blush.

"Yeah, he is and I can tell he likes me, too." My excitement rose and she took notice.

"Calm down, lil sis. Now how can you be so sure he likes you? Boys can be tricky at this age, hell at any age."

"I don't know, Chloe, its in his eyes. Its like we connect when we look at each other." Thinking about Jalen made me smile.

"Aww, now that's love," she teased in a whining tone.

"Shut up, Chloe. See, that's why I don't tell you stuff."

"OK, OK. What's your question? I'm here to help."

"What's my next move?"

"Wait."

"Wait? That's it? Just wait?"

"Yes, you wait for him to move next."

"What if he takes too long?" Now I was worried if I followed her advice I would miss out and never have a boyfriend.

"Trust me, if he really likes you it won't take long at all."

I had to think about Chloe's words carefully and it made a lot of sense. Besides, I'm sure she's had plenty of experience in the boy department being a Senior and all. The way she stays on the phone with Gabriel, she has to know something. He must like her for real to want to talk to her all the time. Before I could even thank her, she was right back where she started.

"Thanks, sis." She just waved me off as returned to face timing with someone who I assumed was Gabriel. I walked out and got halfway down the hallway then I remembered something I needed to ask her. Quickly turning on my heels, I shot back into her room without thinking about knocking.

"Chloe I forgot------" my eyes nearly bucked out of my head making me completely lose my train of thought. She was lying across her bed totally nude taking explicit pictures of herself. When she realized she was caught in the act, the only way she could hide embarrassment was to lash out at me.

"Reecie, what the hell are you doing in here!" Her voice raised an octave as she scrambled to find something to cover herself up.

"I'm sorry, I'm sorry," I apologized repeatedly exiting out the door filled with shame.

"Don't come back in here no more!" She shouted trough the closed door. I felt terrible violating her privacy like that.

Maybe that's what makes boys like girls, showing that you're not afraid to express yourself to them. I'd personally be ashamed to show my body like that, partly because I'm not all the way secure with myself the way she is. Sure my butt was rounding out nicely and I could see the development in my body when I looked at myself naked, but I wasn't ready for anyone else to see me, especially a boy. It would be nice to get a bit more attention, maybe that would make Joi and the others take a step back.

The next day I chose something to wear that fit my curves a little better. I wore a nice Spring top and someting to cover up the jeans I had on, also to hide from my mom who always gave me a full inspection before she drops me off. To my surprise she seemed preoccupied with a call to even take notice.

As soon as I walked down the corridor towards my locker, the stares and heads turned like falling dominoes. I could feel the eyes on me and the attention mounting, yet I never wavered, keeping my stride. In fact, I may have added an extra wiggle to my hips, something I saw my mother do once when we were at the mall, now I see how the guys react. The jeans I was wearing appeared painted on and for the first time in my life I felt a sense of sexiness.

Somebody must've told Jalen because he went out of his way to come down by where my locker was just to get a peek. His locker was nowhere near that area so I'm sure he had to come up with a logical reason for coming my way. The ladies bathroom and water fountain, were at the end of the hallway, my guess was he would play it off and drink up all the water in the tank not to blow his cover. Boys think they're so cool and can be so predictable at times.

Out of the corner of my eye, I saw him approaching. He completely left his crew standing, they were his confidence builders but today he figured he didn't need them.

"Hey Sharice," he said casually as he passed by. It surprised me to hear his voice so clearly over the student traffic. I was glad my back was turned so he couldn't see me blush. My heart beat increased 1000 times over. When I got enough nerve to turn around and speak back, he was gone.

"Who you looking for?" Sasha said noticing the bewildered look on my face. Joi wasn't too far behind her.

"Girl what got into you? Check her out, Sash, she got some "catch me" jeans on." Joi joked. She never hesitated to find humor in a situation.

"There's nothing special about what I have on," I lied as best I could but they read right through it.

"You hear her, Sasha? Reecie, you knew what you were doing when you put that on. If I don't know any better, I'd think you were trying to get your sexy on for Mr. Jalen."

"No I wasn't!" I defended to no avail. Sasha wasn't believing a word I was saying.

"With all that booty poking out, oh yeah, you were definitely trying to get somebody's attention."

"Yall two are tripping."

"Yeah whatever. Well, how come Jalen and his whole crew were up there lurking like vultures when we came over?" Joi pointed out.

The bell rang signaling the next period and it saved my tail from their verbal assault. I grabbed my books then headed to class. Joi and I had American Literature, while Sasha had Pre-calculus. So far the classes have been challenging, a major difference from the school I was at. Having my girls with me has helped with the transition. Now if I can just get my social life together, I'd be alright.

I thought the bell would never ring releasing us from class. American Lit was by far my least favorite subject, I had to wake Joi up twice because Mrs. Stinchcomb was boring us to death. Her slow monotone speech pattern will lull you to sleep. It reminded us of the guy from the 'Dry Eyes' commercial. She may have played the part of the Peanuts school teacher, who sounded just like her.

"Where's Sasha?" I asked Joi, not seeing her come out of her class.

"I don't know, she usually meets us here. Wait, here she comes now, she was in the bathroom." Sasha walked up looking distressed, hair disheveled, head down. She's a fair complexioned girl so her face was very flush.

"What's wrong with you, Sasha?" I asked.

"Yeah, what the hell happened to you, boo?" Joi had no sensitivity. It was obvious something wasn't right with her and I wanted to know what.

"Nothing. I'm good." She tried to mask her disposition but it wasn't working with us, we've known her too long.

"Are you sure?" I looked her in her eyes and saw a lack of confidence, something that wasn't there before. I didn't push though.

A group of girls walked by, headed by Ursula Peters, a tomboyish female who was older than the rest of her peers. She had been kept back a couple years mostly because she skips school on a habitual basis. School officials keep a watch on her due to her activities in and out of school. She has a way of influencing other girls to follow her in cult like fashion, mostly out of fear.

"Bitch!" She spat in our direction, her eyes seethed at Sasha who didn't return her eye contact. "That bitch ain't shit," she mumbled to one of her cohorts as they continued down the hallway in mob.

"What did you do to her, Sasha?" I questioned the whole ordeal and reasoning behind the outburst.

"Nothing," she pleaded with her eyes for us to believe her. "Nothing at all."

Joi interjected, "There has to be a reason why she's hating on you."

"You know me, I don't bother anyone." And she was right. Sasha, as long as I've known her, has always been meek and humble, fun loving, caring and considerate of other people's feelings. She's never loud, rude, or belligerent, how Joi was sometimes, yet she doesn't condemn Joi for being herself. That's just how Sasha was. Always more concerned about her appearance and what people thought about her. She was the pretty one out of us three, the most fashion conscious but never made us feel less than she was. That wasn't her style. If you got to know her, she had a heart of gold.

The voice over the school's intercom system interrupted us, halting everyone in the hallway. I became shocked as well as embarrassed when my name was called to report to the principal's office. My stomach instantly started to get queasy at the thought that I'd might be in trouble, for what I didn't know.

I stepped into the office where an assistant told me to have a seat. The waiting period was like waiting for bad news. My palms were sweating and my heart was beating really fast.

"The Principal will see you now." The assistant called out to me. I knocked on the door nervously.

"Please, come in Ms. Andrews."

"Yes, ma'am." Principal Daniels looked up over her glasses at me.

"Now I don't know what's gotten into you, young lady, but I've been getting complaints about your attire all day. You have attracted a lot of unwanted attention around here and you are treading dangerously close to violating our dress code policy. I'm quite sure your parents wouldn't approve of you coming to school wearing jeans that tight."

"No ma'am, they wouldn't," I said barely above a whisper. "You're not gonna call them, are you?" That was my worst fear.

"I should...but I'm not this time. Consider this your warning." I felt the weight of the world lift off my shoulders. "Let me tell you something, woman to woman, you don't have to wear provocative clothing to gain the attention from boys. That's not the attention you want, trust me on that. Be who you are. You want people to know you from the inside out, not what you show them on the outside. You understand?"

"I understand." I said, feeling like I'd been scolded by a den mother.

"I will call your parents if you come up in my school dressed like that again. Have some standards for yourself."

"I will, ma'am." I left her office feeling empty. When I got to my locker, Joi was waiting to get the scoop like a newscaster. The first thing I noticed, there was no Sasha.

"What was that all about?" She asked, waiting to be in my business

"Nothing too much. Where's Sash?" I quickly changed the subject.

"I don't know. Maybe she's somewhere trying to clear her head. Those girls sounded pretty fierce a while ago."

"I'm worried about her, Joi"

"I know one thing, I wouldn't be too many more "bitches" to them. They'd have to see about me, ya heard?" Joi flexed her imaginary muscles making me chuckle.

"Who do you think you are, Gangsta Boo? You not hard," I snapped her back to reality.

"I'm just saying."

"Well, I'm just saying, we have to keep our girl in prayer. Make sure she gets through whatever's troubling her."

"You sounding more and more like your mom, do you know that?" She meant that to be demeaning I'm sure.

"That's not such a bad thing, if you ask me."

CHAPTER ELEVEN

Adrian

"Did you know he called me?"

"Who?" Cookie inquired hearing the concern in my voice.

"Your husband. He actually had the nerve to call me."

"Are you serious? What could he possibly have to say to you?"

"A lot, evidently. He doesn't like the fact that we talk. He has been monitoring your calls. He's something else."

"Tell me about it. You don't known them half of what I go through."

"I can only imagine."

From the stories she's told me, the abuse has been both mental and emotional. By watching phone records he definitely has a control issue, that leads to deeper problems. He already pays all the bills and even tries to pick out the kinds of clothes she wears, making sure she's appropriately dressed according to his standards.

Confiding in me has helped her cope and built our friendship bond as well. We found out that two people can have a mutual attraction, finding commonalities without the pressure of having sex. Sure we have a sexual nature, we're human beings, but sometimes the friendship can get clouded by misguided emotions.

"Adrian, I'm sorry he reached out to you. Its sad when I feel like I have to hide my phone in my own house."

"Yeah, that's crazy. Its almost how we live in here. It seems as if he has you in a prison, where you're a resident in the house and he's the Warden." She laughed but there was some truth to the statement.

"I wish I could tell you he won't bother you any more but he's unpredictable and honestly I don't know what he's capable of doing."

"You're right. If he treats you that way and you're his wife, he probably don't give a damn about me."

"Well, if its any consolation, I care about you," she said in a sweet voice.

"Thank you, Cookie. I care about you too. I just have two concerns."

"And what's that?"

"What are you gonna do when I get out of here? And how are you gonna handle your situation with Pastor Andrews? Because its plain to see that even if you wanted to leave, he's not gonna let you go peacefully."

"I'll figure something out." That's all I needed to hear.

I ended the call with Cookie, mainly because there was a disturbance in the dorm. I don't like involving her in certain things that happen on the inside. The first thing I needed to do was secure my phone. Even though I was engrossed in a conversation with Cookie, my surroundings were top priority. Once I tended to my business, I laid back on my bunk. In a hostile environment, the best thing to do was to stay out of the way. Prison heightens your awareness, putting the senses back to work. Listening becomes your most valued asset.

I've learned over the years that if it ain't your business, don't make it your business. So I sat back and listened to the commotion take place. The noise level escalated when more people got involved in the fracas. Some of the leaders in the dorm like JoJo, Tree, and Richie Rich, made their way to the area trying to maintain order.

"I know you been telling, nigga!" A voice boomed from the back. "You a snitch and can't nobody tell me different. I got word from my people that its been you that had us getting shook down left and right. Playing that fake ass church role, I'm not buying it. You may be fooling these people around here but not me." One Time snapped out. He was relatively new to our dorm but he'd been through the last two major shakedowns we've had and took a loss both times. Once with his phone then right behind that with a good amount of dope.

After hearing his tirade, I wondered what facts he had to substantiate calling whoever a snitch. That's a strong allegation and in prison you had to have proof. Labels will travel fast if spoken by the right person and it will stick from dorm to dorm, camp to camp. There's really no escaping the snitch label once its put in the air. Unless you have concrete references from your side, whom are in veteran status in the system, that's the only way to reverse the stigma.

The man tried to plead his case quietly hoping the conversation wouldn't be heard by too many. The dorm elders were quiet, only listening to One Time's interrogation. The voices rose to a level heard all the way in the day room area, it was enough to draw a crowd away from the television just to see what was going on. I sat up in my bed and watched because crowds usually brought unwanted attention. And sure enough it did.

"12-12-12!" Somebody yelled out alerting that the officers were coming in to check things out. At this point One Time was tired of talking and was ready for action.

"Hold on, One Time, put the shank down!" Now I heard Richie Rich's voice for the first time. He knew his potential and the end result wouldn't be pretty. "We got too much to lose in here" Rich pleaded.

"Hell, messing with this snitching ass nigga, we gonna keep losing. I might as well do him and take one for the team. I got 50 years to the door, so what I got to lose?" He spat out. JoJo tried his best to negotiate with One Time.

"Look brah, we can handle this another way. How

about we just put him out the dorm." The officers were treading close after making rounds.

"Naw man, putting him on the door won't do nothing. He'll just go somewhere else and snitch them out." One Time explained.

"I ain't no snitch!" The voice shouted out causing the officers to take notice. I recognized the voice but couldn't believe it was him in the middle of this.

When the two officers moved through the crowd and saw One Time with the shank pointed at the defenseless man, they reacted. "We have a 10-10 in progress!" One shouted in his radio. Moments later there was a flood of officers pouring through the front door of the dorm.

"Everybody back up!" Sergeant Davis ordered as he arrived on the scene. One Time didn't flinch. By this time he was ready to go.

"Hey get him off me! He's sticking me!" The high pitched shrills made me get up now knowing exactly who it was being attacked. I made my way over to the dispersed crowd and saw blood puddling every where. It took three officers to apprehend One Time because he was a big man. One had to wrestle the knife away because he was still trying to get some licks in. They were finally able to cuff him then take him out.

Two more officers picked up the other man, who was face down holding his bloody side. Getting him on his feet, our eyes met as they carried him out. It was my partner, Preacher Man. The look he gave me was scary.

"I ain't no snitch," he mumbled under his weakened breath. "I ain't no snitch, Adrian." He wanted me to believe him, and I did. I knew him probably better than anyone else. His character didn't show him to be anything other than an aspiring man of God. I'm not the type to go by what others say, I base my decisions on how I experience someone. Preach has been well respected in the dorm for as long as I've been here. I hate that something like that happened to him. Some will probably question where I was and why I didn't try to help him since we were so close, I honestly didn't know what was going on.

 I made a choice to stay in my lane which meant not getting mixed up in stuff that would bring more harm than good. What nobody in the dorm knew was that I was about to go home. For that reason, I primarily chose to distance myself. After all these years, the single most important thing to me was starting my new life outside these walls. I watched as they put Preacher Man on the medical cart, who knew what his future was going to be. I'm sure his faith would carry him through, however, that won't keep him from being tested by the ways of prison. Incarceration has a way of making the mightiest men weak and men who seem weak stronger than most. Preach was one of those whose meekness was mistaken for weakness. Maybe not now but the truth will come out or maybe not. I won't be around to see it.

"Adrian, I didn't know." Pam tried to reasoning as I stepped into her office to clean out the trash. She wanted me to stay and talk but I had way too much to do, plus it was mid-morning and we had a lobby full of people. Tuesday was counseling inmate intake day. The new arrivals to the camp had to get classified with counselors. For me, I had to organize appointments, pass out paperwork, and then make their individual films folders in addition to my normal duties.

"Didn't know what?" I quickly answered continuing to move through her office efficiently collecting papers that needed to be shredded.

"That you're going home. I'm so happy for you. It has to be exciting to know that you're finally leaving this place." She expressed.

"I'm still processing it all. Just trying to stay focused. Time is still moving and I'm here in the moment." I downplayed my response.

I went back into the lobby area to see who was next to meet with the counselor. When I looked up, two of the black suited security team members and Sgt. Davis were coming through the door.

"Upshaw, we need to talk to you." Sarge announced making everyone notice. This wasn't the first time they've come by my detail questioning me about something, I just wondered what it was this time. My fear was that someone had written a kite about my dealings with Ms. Breston. Guys get infatuated by her pretty face, nice body and how friendly she was. They'll use that as motivation to get me out the way.

Pam stepped out hearing the voices, Sgt. Davis gave

her a broad smile as if she was the most beautiful this moving, he was always happy to be in her presence.

"Is there something I can help you with, Sgt." Just the sound of her saying his title aloud made him puff his bulky chest out some more.

"I need to speak with your orderly about a matter, nothing to worry your pretty little self about." He was grinning out of control. "Is there somewhere we can go to talk?" He was just as nice and polite.

"Its your world, take your pick of any office." She said casually not trying to feed in to his flirts.

"Let's go, Upshaw, we can go in the conference room." The counselors who were in there came out immediately seeing Sgt. Davis and his henchmen.

"Have a seat." I did as he said giving him a blank stare.

"Look, I'm gonna get right to the point, we got a call about you. Do you know a Sandra Andrews?" I had to be careful how I answered because I didn't know what they knew. "Never mind, I don't even want you to answer. It will piss me off if you lie. Pastor Carlton Andrews is well respected here at Lofton State Prison, so when we get informed that he suspects one of our inmates has been communicating with his wife, we have to look into it."

"Now, Upshaw, you've never given us any trouble and we're aware that you're going home real soon so I'd sure hate to ruin your parole date by taking up charges on you for possession of contraband." One of the goons threatened.

"Oh, don't look so surprised, we're quite sure if we

search the dorm we'll find the phone you're been using to talk to the First Lady." Sgt. Davis had his ducks in a row leaving me no room to speak. There was nothing to be said. The other one spoke.

"The First Lady of the church, man? Out of all the women you could get with, you chose the Pastor's wife? Boy I hope you know what you're getting into." He stated.

"I know what he will be getting into if he keeps playing with fire." Sarge interjected. "A pine box, cause that man is gonna kill him when he gets outta here." They all found humor in my dark time. "So I'm gonna let this serve as your warning, cause I like you kid. This stays between us in this room. Just leave that man's wife alone."

His word resonated in my head. I had a plan but it may have to change when I get out. Carl went to great lengths to get my attention. Well he got it. I just wonder how much of a problem he'll be when I'm on the other side of the fence.

CHAPTER TWELVE

Cookie

Just waking up in the morning, gotta thank God.
I dont know but today seems kinda odd.
No barking from the dogs, no smog.
And momma cooked the breakfast with no hog.

THE SOUND OF ICE CUBE'S GRUFF VOCE WAS MY ALARM clock this morning. Ever since I've been sleeping in Chloe's room there's no telling what I may awaken to. The girls and I worked out an agreement that I could sleep in either one of their rooms in exchange for more freedom. They're good girls, now maturing into young women and I am their example of what a woman should be.

Its a shame that they have to see division between Carl and I. For the sake of them, I'm trying desperately to work our marital problems, however the emotional void is breaking me down slowly. When I looked at myself in the mirror, there was weight gain on my body and darkness around my eyes. When a woman's beauty starts to decline, her self worth wasn't too far behind. In order to restore some of what I've lost, changes have to be made.

The first thing I was seeking was peace, so leaving our bedroom was easy because there definitely wasn't any peace there. Of course Carl didn't like me sleeping in another bed, he felt married couples should sleep in the same room, in a conventional world that may be the case, but our marriage was hardly conventional.

I went and looked in Reecie's room, she must've gotten a ride to school from her father. That was usually my job in the morning and he would pick her up in the afternoon but for some reason Carl feels like he has to compete with me when it comes to parenting. This was something we're supposed to be doing together not against each other. Ever since the girls were little, he's always tried to gain favor with them over me. He won that battle with Chloe but I be damned if he pulled my baby girl into his wicked ways.

I had a nine o'clock appointment with one of the most difficult patients. Even though I love helping people, some of the work I do takes a real toll on me, which makes it hard to talk about it. Carl's so wrapped up with business at the church, we rarely sit down and discuss work. Normally couples end their day with a recap of their days events, however like I mentioned before, we are far from normal.

When I stepped out the front door, it seemed like the sun was shining unusually bright today. The neighborhood was serene, all that was heard was faint sounds of birds chirping a tune and early morning lawn mowers humming. The air was fresh and I took a second to take it in before getting in the car. I headed down the road bobbing my head to the radio, even my favorite song was playing. Today just might be a good day.

"Be Optimistic" was what Ann Nesby was singing which put me in a pretty positive mood, that was until I pulled up to Mrs. Santos' house. By being a home nurse, I'll never know what I'll encounter when I visit a patient. Mrs. Santos was one of those patients I didn't look forward to, that's why I scheduled her first thing in the morning. Once I got through those two hours, the rest of the day was a breeze.

When she opened the door the smell of pet hairs infiltrated my nostrils like DEA agents on a raid, kicking my nasal passage down rendering me helpless. She had an obscene amount of cats that polluted her house. It was a wonder how she didn't have anymore health issues than the ones she had. Hell, I was surprised I didn't develop some just by being there taking care of her.

Mrs. Santos was also an extremely large woman. The last time I did her vital signs and checked her weight, she was crossing the 400lb mark. Her husband used to be her primary caregiver before he passed away suddenly. His loss triggered her weight gain, leaving her almost bedridden, which made my job harder. At first my responsibilities were basic, clean up to make sure the place was disinfected, make sure she had an early meal, and also keep her bedpan changed, which was the most disgusting part.

There were other nurses who were to relieve me for the remainder of the day, basically giving round the clock care. I believe I cursed myself by performing my duties a little too well because she started requesting me personally. Luckily I had a full compliment of patients so she had to settle for someone else.

In addition to the filth I had the pleasure of cleaning, Mrs. Santos was very demanding. There's nothing worse than a 400lb woman barking orders from a bed for two hours. The cats made it that much worse. Everywhere I stepped were cats. Brown ones. Orange ones. Black ones with white on their tails. White ones with black around their eyes. There were even kittens which meant some breeding was going on somewhere around there that she didn't know about.

After my two hour torture session, I had an appointment with Mr. Deanty, a paraplegic from Jamaica. He was 70 years old with a wonderful sense of humor. For a man who will never walk again, he still continued to live a quality life. His first name was Richie but I like to call him Mr. Rich because he was rich in spirt as well as money. I always enjoyed his company as he did mine.

My phone rang as I left Mr. Rich's house, the screen read 'restricted', I answered anyway.

"Hello"

"Its just a matter of time. I'm gonna get you or somebody close to you." The gravely sounding voice was haunting. They hung up as quickly as they called in, disturbing my peace. I couldn't even utter a word. It took me a few moments to process what has just happened. The threat sounded real, but where did it come from. The stop light allowed me an opportunity to regroup. My screen lit up again which frightened me to look. I answered with aggression this time.

"Look, whoever this is, I don't care about your threats!" I barked into the phone.

"Cookie, this is Maxine." I took a second glance to make sure. Putting her on speaker, I kept driving.

"Girl, hey."

"Who in the world were you just talking to? Cause it was obvious it wasn't me. You sounds like you were ready to tear somebody's head off."

"A prank caller just threatened me then hung up. The coward, I thought they were calling back but it was you."

"I'm so glad you weren't mad at me, you got a little gangster in you, girl."

"I haven't always been in the church, Max." I admitted

"Who did you think it was?" She asked.

"I don't have a clue, I'm just worried about my family, he threatened them too, and sounded serious."

"What did they say?"

"I'm gonna get you and anybody close to you, something like that." I repeated.

"That does sound serious." She stated the obvious.

"I know one thing, I'm not gonna stop living. I serve God not man."

"I know that's right, Amen to that. Anyway, I wanted to tell you I talked to my son."

"Torry, right? Isn't he out in California?"

"San Francisco, actually. He works for the Bureau."

"The FBI?" I knew that was a stupid question as soon as I asked it.

"Yes. He's out there on assignment. I had him checking on some options for me with my case. Even though he's federal, he has connections with the state. When I mentioned to him about the perjury case pending, he vowed to do whatever he could to keep me out of jail."

"That's a good son."

"Yeah, the best. So, he started doing research on those guys, seeing if they had a history. Drugs and violence is what he came up with."

"Well, we definitely know those two were on their résumé." I joked. "Did he give you any strategy?"

"All he told me was that he had an ace in the hole and not to worry." She stated.

"Don't worry, huh? That's easy to say way over on the West Coast. He must have a helluva trick up his sleeve. There's a lot to worry about, Max."

"I know. But I don't have much of a choice. He's the only one really offering me help. The lawyer is supposed to be compiling information but she doesn't sound too confident."

" I just hope he doesn't leave you out to dry. I'm not trying to visit you in jail, Max."

"I hope not either. I'm not built for jail, way too cute for that." She laughed but could tell she was concerned. There was an uncomfortable silence.

"On a lighter note, you know my friend is coming home soon." I offered.

"Which friend is this?"

"Adrian, the one in prison. He told me he's on his way out." My excitement couldn't be masked.

"Wow that's crazy. Are you ready for that? Doesn't sound like good news, sounds like an additional problem. But you genuinely sound happy."

"Max, I am. I know there will be some issues I have to resolve but I'm willing to do it."

"Well, I'm happy for you. But you do have some things to figure out and you better get on it quick. You don't want one situation unfinished before you start another."

"Truthfully, I really don't know how to feel. My emotions are swirling. On the inside, he was safe from me and all my drama, now the whole thing can be touched. I've tried to conceive every scenario but I honestly don't know how its all gonna play out."

"This should be interesting. I'm glad I have a ring-side seat. I'll keep some days open for counseling. I have a feeling you'll be in giving me updates." We both laughed at her realness.

I hung up with Max wondering what was going on in

her mind. She was dealing with a lot. Her tone was full of skepticism. To tell the truth I'd be skeptical too if the shoe were on the other foot. I'm glad she stayed objective. Sometimes friends can say the wrong thing at the wrong time. I'm sure I have her support either way it goes. I have no clue which way this will go. Right now, I'm following my heart, while at the same time, chasing happiness.

CHAPTER THIRTEEN

Carl

AFTER THE MERRY GO ROUND CONVERSATION I HAD with Adrian, I realized he really wasn't the problem, their affair, if you want to call it that, was a result of our marital issues. For whatever reason, Sandra feels more comfortable talking with him rather than me. That's her power of choice, however marriages are full of ups and downs, many choices are made between husband and wife. In this case she chose her path without me.

Since she has decided to entertain conversations with Adrian, I have some decisions to make myself. My lawyer and I spoke about my situation and what kind of options I had. He suggested I do something radical, something to get her attention. I didn't necessarily agree but what did I have to lose. At this point my marriage was on thin ice and was shattering at every turn.

When she comes home, I was going to grant her the freedom she desires. Whether she's said it or not, actions speak louder than words. We haven't slept together intimately in I don't know how long. In fact, we don't even sleep in the same room anymore and that's disheartening for husband to see his wife becoming detached. We've been together so long I can tell when things are different.

Maybe things would've gotten better if I had taken her up on going to counseling. Maybe I should've listened more or paid more attention so I could've seen the change in her earlier. Maybe its not her at all, it could be me. Either way, in order to move forward we need to identify what our issue is, then go our separate ways if that's what it has come to. I'm gonna put the ball in her court.

Sandra came home, put her things down like she's had a long day, then retreated to the kitchen where the girls were at the table. At least, there wasn't tension in the room.

"Hey guys," I entered the room in a jovial mood.

"Hello, dad," Reecie answered without looking up from something she was into on her phone. Chloe was also engrossed in her phone and gave me a quick wave. Sandra didn't speak at all. It looked as if her mind was somewhere else, or she may have been faking. I really wasn't trying to discuss anything with her in front of the girls. They've witnessed enough of us arguing, I can only imagine what kind of perception they have of us.

"Sandra, when you get a minute, can I have a word with you?" I asked politely. She paused then finally acknowledged me.

"What is it would you like to talk about?" Her eye focused on mine but I could see where the love had gone elsewhere.

"In private please." I left out hoping she would follow. Going up the stairs, I peeked behind me surprised to see her coming.

When we got to what used to be our bedroom, I began to speak. She cut me off with whatever had been brewing on her mind.

"What did you get out of calling Adrian?"

"Excuse me?" The question caught me off guard. I wasn't expecting to address it but since she went there, I was game.

"You know what I'm talking about and don't act like you didn't go through my phone records to get the number. I know you, Carl. I believe you missed your calling, instead of a Pastor you should've been a private investigator."

"That's low, Sandra." I responded.

"What you're doing is low, Carl. The way you move, snooping around, waltzing around the church like you're high and mighty, like your shit don't stink. There's a lot going on that church, good and bad. Whatever happens in there is solely on you yet it affects both of us. And I can tell you this with all honesty, you make it very hard to be First Lady."

"What about my wife? Is it difficult to be my wife too?" I asked the loaded question expecting to hear the worst. What I got was silence. She finally spoke but went in another direction.

"I want to know why you felt the need to call that man?" She returned there.

"Because he is cheating with my wife!" I blurted out with volume.

"Now, do you know how foolish you sound? I didn't known it was against the law to have male friends. And I didn't know you would be so controlling that you wouldn't want me talking to anyone else especially another man."

"It may not be against the law to have male friends but I'm sure its not lawful to talk to man incarcerated on a daily basis." I made sure she knew I knew how regular she'd been talking to him. "So since we're on that, is this thing with Adrian something you plan on continuing?" She hit me where it hurt so I had no problem doing the same. Her silence was enough of an answer for me.

"I don't know." She uttered out finally and for once I got a truthful answer out of her.

"You don't know? Wow, that's exactly what I wanted to hear from my wife. Let me get this straight, what you and this Adrian fellow are doing doesn't constitute infidelity to you?" The question was as direct as I could put it.

"Like I said before, he's a good friend and has been a huge help to me when times were tough." She explained.

"Is your life really that tough, Sandra? You have everything you could want. I provide you with whatever you need. Our lifestyle is far from tough."

"Everything ain't financial, Carl, it's an obvious lack of emotional commitment going on here."

"And you think consorting with a convicted felon will fill that emotional void?" I swung where it would hurt on purpose.

"Its better than consorting with someone who doesn't understand how to love. Our relationship hasn't had that element in a long time, Carl, and its a shame that I had to talk to another man to figure that out." Her statement stung and raised up an ire within me.

"I believe you would screw that man if you had the chance. Hell, in your mind you probably already have." Sandra gave me a cold stare, one that I've never seen before. She looked at me as if she didn't even know me and at that moment I knew we were at the point of no return.

"You know what, Carl? If I were to dignify that statement with a response it would be disrespectful, more disrespectful than what you just insinuated. So I'll save what I really want to say-------"

"Say what's on your mind, Sandra" I interjected now looking to ignite the fire.

"Don't push me, Carl, you may not like the results." She rebuffed.

"I'm a big boy, try me." She took a deep breath then took a step towards me.

"Carl, for the longest time you've loved that church more than you've loved me, even more then you've loved God. With all the elaborate sermons, missions, and fancy suits only distracts people from them big picture."

"Enlighten me, Sandra, what exactly is the big picture?" I was curious at this point.

"You want the congregation and the community to revere you as if you're God. Control feeds you. Your ego is dependent upon how people perceive you. This quest for control over the people has turned you into a different person." I was shocked to hear her speak to me in this manner.

"I haven't changed, Sandra." I defended.

"Sure you have, you just don't realize it because you're constantly evolving. How you've been living hasn't allowed you to see yourself differently." She explained very clearly. But wasn't making sense to me at all.

"From the beginning, its always been about you. Whatever goes on at the church has to reflect Pastor Andrews in a certain way. The First Lady has to dress in this manner in order to make a favorable impression to the public. That's why you made sure you ordered me specific clothes and hats to wear. Nothing the kids do can bring shame on the church , or you particularly, that would be detrimental to this grand persona you've built up. You, old husband of mine, are larger than life itself. Keep in mind, you have children who look at you in this light, the light you project."

"Is this light so bad for them?' I asks her.

"Its bad if the light isn't leading them anywhere."

"Are you lead by this light, Sandra?" I needed to know where she stood.

"Carl, your light doesn't shine bright enough for me to follow you." She took the gloves off and was swinging blows like haymakers.

"And what you're doing is befitting a First Lady?"

"I'm not caught up in titles. Besides you're the one fighting allegations of infidelity, with a man at that." She had to bring that up.

"I told you about that situation, I wasn't cheating with no man." I was sick and tired of defending myself.

"Hey, its not me you have to prove yourself to. Your skeletons are the ones falling out of the closet, not mine. I have nothing to hide from the congregation, do you? And what about this son of yours? Sister Allen told me how he ran off with the offering drop." I didn't have a thing to say because I was still processing it. "Yet another thing WE have to deal with as Pastor and First Lady. Did I ask to be in it? Nope, but because we're attached automatically, people will associate me with you. So this whole discussion about whether I'm cheating or not is irrelevant. If anything, the affair is on you and all you have going on in that church. If I could I would separate myself from the whole thing." Her words came at me like a cold glass of water splashed in my face. When I asked her to talk, I was prepared for the worst, nothing this cold.

"Look over there on your side of the bed" I told her pointing to where she used to sleep. There was a legal sized envelope laying on the pillow with her name on it.

"What is this?" She asked picking it up.

"Your separation papers." I walked out of the room without giving her a chance to respond. I gave her some time and space to read over what my lawyer had prepared. With everything I had heard, she was basically asking for it. I just made it easier for her. If she chooses to exit then we can do it amicably.

As I went down the stairs, I saw that I had several missed texts in my phone from my friend at the Prince Georges County police department. I alerted Detective Bryant to the events that happened at the church. He took down my report regarding Carl Jr. I even explained to him I had hired him to do a job. The first thing Det. Bryant wanted to ensure that it wasn't an inside set up. After I clarified why I hired him as opposed to going with my usual contractor, he said he would treat it as a robbery. Carl Jr. was now a suspect. I had to head down to the station to meet with the Detective. The money was insured but it was the principal of it being stolen that needed to be handled. So I pressed formal charges on Carlton Andrews Jr., if that was in fact his real name.

CHAPTER FOURTEEN

The Watchers

THEY SAT AT THE TOP OF THE HILL FACING THE entrance of the neighborhood. The nondescript, light grey sedan made it easy for them to blend in. All the cars coming and going could be seen from their vantage point. This team had one mission: keep watch on the Andrews woman and anyone with her. There was another team assigned to Maxine Stinson, the therapist who stuck her nose in the wrong business. She's the reason everyone was on alert, all she had to do was the right thing and sleeping would be a whole lot easier.

Pappo wanted this situation under control, the longer it lingered the more uncomfortable he got. How he looked at it, those two women were responsible for substantial money loss. Not only that but his nephew, Richie Rich, was no closer to coming home. Maxine Stinson was paid to do a deed and didn't fulfill her obligation. The money she was paid had to be returned to him or else there will be repercussions.

He had different reasons for wanting Sandra Andrews. Even though both women stole money from him, the way she did it was totally disrespectful. She actually had the gumption to come to one of his stash houses and pull off a robbery. He even lost a couple good men in the process which fueled Pappo to increase his manpower in search of her. But he knew she didn't act alone, that's why he extended his efforts to finding Gabriel Measures too.

Rico was the new man on the team and Pappo's youngest nephew. He had a heart of gold at times then it could turn cold as ice in the blink of an eye. That's the kind of sinister trait Pappo was looking for. He had a hot temper but it was understandable, he was young and eager to please his uncle. Rico was willing to do anything and that's what prompted Pappo to bring him on, also because he had a connection to Gabriel Measures.

It was very important to Pappo to get everyone involved in the robbery caper that cost him almost a hundred grand. He had a read on Sandra Andrews, it was just a matter of time for her, but Gabriel Measures was high on his list because he killed one of his good men and seriously injured another. Pappo with the help of his nephews, vowed to strike revenge on each of them, one by one.

He had an inside track on Gabriel, also known as Game. The name Game was given to the young go-getter mostly because of his basketball prowess however, for the Crawford family, Game's street reputation had been a constant thorn in their side. Rico knew him all too well due to their association in the drug trade, the also just so happened to attend the same high school. Although it was short lived when Rico took the term "high" in high school literally. He thought everyone there should've been on the same sort of drug. He ultimately was expelled for illegally dealing narcotics on school grounds. Ironically, Gabriel was doing the same, however his basketball stardom masked his activities.

Ever since then, there has been an unspoken jealousy and competition between the two. Both were workers for a larger operation but in their minds they had something to prove and pride was a prime motivator for each to make a name for themselves. In the street, Rico had the upper hand. His uncle Pappo had all the connections and Rico was always eager to let people know that he came from a made family. Game was one who relied on his own reputation to get by, he too had people behind him but his team wasn't as strong as Rico's.

Pappo and Rico did a stakeout at the Andrews residence, making sure Sandra Andrews doesn't travel anywhere without them knowing. Rico and his right hand man, Amari, were paired together while Pappo's other nephew Demani had his own crew tailing Dr. Maxine Stinson. He would take them each at his own time, saving Gabriel for last.

"I see a car coming this way," Rico radioed to Pappo

who was holed up in the safe house strategizing. He was the type to never let his left hand know what his right was doing, not even his nephews.

"Make sure its her," Pappo responded.

"The car came out of the driveway, its coming past me but its not her, its the Pastor. What you want me to do? Follow him?" Pappo had to pause before he answered.

"No let him go, we want the wife."

"10-4" Rico confirmed.

Meanwhile, on the other side of town, Maxine was seen exiting the grocery store. Demani had been following her closely from home to the cleaners, when she filled her car with gas and now they sat in the parking lot giving her a little space before they pulled out behind her. Demani and his crew stayed at least a car's length from Maxine ensuring that they stayed inconspicuous. She seemed oblivious the way she swayed back and forth to the music she listened to.

When Pappo issued a threat to her son Torry, he thought that would be enough to make her come clean with the money she owed. At first his plan was to use her son as collateral to force a move but his work transferred him to the West Coast which made it a bit more difficult to apprehend him. With that leverage lost, Pappo had to change his plans.

Demani was driving an all black utility van with tinted windows to conceal his identity. He was becoming extremely impatient chasing this woman around town. If

Pappo would let him, he would have already snatched her up and delivered her to his uncle instead of playing this cat and mouse game. It wasn't his call so he continued to follow the rules of engagement Pappo set out.

"I have the Stinson woman in my sights." Demani radioed.

"Good. Good. Keep a close watch on her but do not engage until I say, got it? Pappo ordered in his raspy tone.

"Got it." Demani hated taking orders even if was from his uncle. He had gotten to the age where he thought he should be calling shots. To his uncle Pappo, Demani really hadn't earned the right to lead without guidance, however for a young understudy hearing that he wasn't ready, was not a consideration.

A call came from Rico just as Pappo ended radio traffic with Demani.

"I think I have her, Unc. Another car is heading my way fitting the description of her car." Rico reported.

"You can't think, son, you have to be sure its her. Every detail is vital when doing this." Pappo explained.

"Its her, Unc, they just passed me."

"Who is they? She isn't alone?" Pappo was curious now.

"Its the Andrews lady but she has a young girl with her." Rico detailed. That must be her daughter, Pappo presumed. From the Intel he had collected, Sandra Andrews, the First Lady of Victory in Faith Baptist

Church, was married with two daughters, one adopted, one biological. His wheels began to turn and a slow smile crept on his face. He enjoyed the thought that graced his mind.

"Follow them and don't let them out of your sight."

CHAPTER FIFTEEN

Adrian

"Warden is on the walk!" Someone hollered out over the normal dormitory noise.

"Where is he at?" Another one asked aloud hoping to get a head start on whatever contraband he needed to hide.

"Coming in! Coming in!" JoJo was standing by as lookout before he scurried to the back of the living area with the rest of the people in the day room.

Everybody lined up by their respective beds awaiting whatever speech the Warden came with. He was accompanied by his usual security detail as well as the Captain. For his safety, he always traveled with an entourage, he never knew who may have had a vendetta against him.

"Where is inmate Spencer?" He asked breaking the silence.

He was referring to David Spencer or D. Spence as he liked to be called by us. D. Spence was one of the few white boys that was well respected by everyone, especially the black and Hispanic inmates mainly because he was a move maker. A move maker is a guy who is able to make things happen for the benefit of himself and others, mostly through trafficking or sales.

David Spencer had made his way by catching the attention of a willing female officer who was down on her luck. She carried out one task for him which brought her enough money to pique her curiosity and motivate her to do it again and again. The money ended up being too easy to turn down, soon they became each others main source of income. She was making so much on the side by trafficking contraband for David that her check was secondary.

As the saying goes, nothing lasts forever. The female officer he had at his previous institution finally got questioned for illegal dealings with an inmate. Both of them had all their bases covered and nothing was able to be proven so the institution had no alternative but to hault the investigation and the allegations. Instead of working under those circumstances, she chose to resign, while David opted to ask for a hardship transfer, citing that he had a terminally ill relative he needed to be close to. The facility went for it, granting him his wishes.

With the amount of tax free money they amassed, it was easy for them to walk away. In his eyes, they were ahead of the game so he didn't mind starting over somewhere else. When he arrived at Lofton his reputation traveled with him. Other inmates know when they're in the presence of chain gang legends and that's what D.

Spence was considered, a legend. He was known for having a commissary account full of money, almost $10,000 and even more in an account on the street controlled by his longtime girlfriend.

She was so loyal to him that she knew what he was up to on the inside and she still supported him. In fact, she encouraged his hustle by reinvesting his money in more product. He liked the woman who helped him make thousands upon thousands yet he loved the woman who kept all his money straight.

"Yeah, I'm over here," I heard D. Spence answer the Warden in a callous tone. I couldn't see him but I could only imagine the look of disgust on the Warden's face hearing how he was addressed.

"Yeah?" One of the security officers approached David. "You don't answer your Warden in that manner."

"He's your Warden, not mine." He said smugly. My mouth dropped at how D. Spence talked to them.

"Where is he at?" The Warden stepped into the cut where D. Spence slept. "Step out for a minute, son" he ordered to Spencer's bunkmate so he could get closer to him. "Now you listen, Mr. Spencer, I know all about you. I read your profile and I have to admit you're pretty good at what you do. However, at my prison, that's not quite good enough." D. Spence gave him a smirk

"Just give me a little time to get warmed up then I can show you some things."

"You think this is all fun and games, Spencer?" The Warden's tone rose a notch. "It's a game you will not win."

"Oh, I'm already winning. I told you just let me get warmed up but really I'm already warm. Courtesy of your prison, I'm already up $6000, when this next drop hits in ah... 15 minutes," he looked at his very expensive watch. "Then I'll be up another five grand." The Warden turned a shade of red that wasn't even in the crayon box.

"Get him out of here!" The Warden shouted to his team now thoroughly embarrassed. "I still win Spencer. You won't get any more money out of my facility. I'm putting you on the bus immediately!" D. Spence laughed at his threat.

"Doesn't matter where you send me, the money will still be made. This was just a money stop anyway. It has started here and will be moving long after I leave. Things are already in place, the wheels are in motion. Choo Choo!" D. Spence made the train noise on his way out the door in arrogant fashion.

"Get that inmate out of here now!" The Warden's ire was all the way to his highest level. "And you guys, find that package! I don't care what we have to do just find it. I don't want any excuses." The Warden stormed out without even dismissing us. We all busted out laughing when they were out of earshot. It wouldn't have surprised me if D. Spence sent them on a wild goose chase. There probably wasn't even a package to be found.

The legend of David Spencer continued. His story travels with him and this saga was just another notch on his belt. Soon the story turned to a tall tale. The money told in the story went from $6000 to $10,000 then to

$20,000 , the more the tale was told, the more it spread. We just laughed when it came back to us because we knew the truth.

"Upshaw, report to counseling," the voice on the intercom echoed throughout the dorm. I haven't been back to detail since the goon squad came in there questioning me about he Pastor's wife. After that day, I chose to take a break from work and stay out of the limelight. Working up front had me in the line of fire, I'd rather be out of sight and out of mind.

I wondered why they were calling me. Not showing up to work should've told them that I wasn't interested in being there. Yet I also knew that without an official schedule change they could call me whenever they felt like it. Against my wishes, I got dressed and went to work. There was no telling what I was walking into.

Pam was coming out of the big conference room when I arrived. She had an arm full of file folders and when saw me her eyes avoided mine.

"What's up?" I asked nonchalantly. She continued walking towards her office then stopped in from of me.

"What's up with you? I'm hearing a lot of things about you," she had a hint of attitude. I wasn't quite sure what she heard but I didn't bite the bait.

"This is Lofton State Prison, there's always somebody saying something. Inmate.com is out of control around here."

"Oh, it wasn't something an inmate said?" Now I was curious. I tried to throw her off with a bit of humor.

"Well, whatever you heard it isn't true."

"Answer this for me, why would the Sgt. and his goons have to come up in here cuff you up, then question you about messing with someone's wife?" The conversation just changed dramatically. The look of hurt was written all over her face. "Your silence is enough to tell me its true."

"See, there you go."

"What? Would you like to explain yourself?" I stepped all the way inside her office.

"Its not what you think." I started with the classic cliché.

"Why do men always say that when they've messed up? Please say something original."

"OK, look, yes they were right about me talking to Ms. Andrews."

"Don't you mean, Mrs. Andrews? She is married right?"

"Yes she is. Our conversations were mostly of the counseling nature. She's going through a lot and needed an objective ear." I tried to explain.

"An objective ear huh? OK Mr. Counselor, how did you come in contact with her?" At this point I knew all her questions would be loaded.

"At church."

"Church?" She laughed. "So while you've been praising the Lord, you were working on your macking skills."

"It really wasn't like that, Pam. Our meeting wasn't planned. Church was a place we both just happened to be at."

"And you made a choice to pursue her," she filled in. "Let me guess, you were talking to her on the phone that I got for you?" She asked already knowing the answer.

"Pam, there's nothing I can tell you to make is sound better. We're friends. I don't see where that's a problem." I stated boldly.

"If you don't see a problem then its obvious we aren't where I thought we were. Damn, Adrian, were you just using me or what?" Now that hurt.

"No, Pam, how can you say that?"

"Because things were changing and I couldn't put my finger on it. I can see now that your attention has been elsewhere. I wondered why our phone conversations have lessened but I never said anything. The truth eventually comes out. I'm not mad at you though." The sudden change in attitude scared me.

"You're not?"

"No not at all. You're a man. You may find this hard to believe but I've dealt with men who didn't appreciate a good thing before."

"I do appreciate you, Pam," I expressed trying to salvage whatever was left of what we had.

"You sure have a way of showing it." Her eyes showed her disappointment.

"Look, men do a lot of dumb shit and I'd be a fool to sit here trying to get you to believe me. But our relationship is different."

"You mean different than the one you have with her?"

"Different period. What we have doesn't compare." It seemed like my words were getting to her.

"Adrian, I'm taking a huge risk messing with you, I told you that from the beginning. You've got my feelings involved and my concern is what are we gonna do when you hit the streets?" How was I supposed to answer that. What did she know because I'm not sure what my plans will be.

"As a counselor I'd like to be sure that you won't return to this place. As someone who loves you, I need to know where your heart lies." She shocked me with the love talk.

"You love me, Pam?" I asked.

"Of course I do, I'm about to be the mother of your child."

CHAPTER SIXTEEN
Reecie

AND THEN EVERYTHING WENT BLACK ...

My girls met me at the entrance when mom dropped me off at the school. It was the ritual that bonded us, the proverbial coffee that started our day. We always smiled as we greeted each other. There was an unspoken understanding that we needed this friendship as a compass to navigate us through this journey in our adolescent lives.

Joi was her usual jovial self, teasing and joking as we walked towards our lockers. Sasha, on the other hand, was a bit quiet and distant. We could see it on her eyes not to mention her posture reflected a certain weakness. It appeared that something had damaged her, but as her friend we didn't show her that we noticed the change, just handled her with care. Eventually she'll come around.

Leave it to Joi to pull off the kid gloves and at track the throat. "Girl, what's been eating at you?" She asked Sasha out of nowhere. Of course, all I could do was roll my eyes at her insensitivity, she always knew the wrong things to say at the inappropriate times. "You haven't been your self lately." Joi continued.

"I'm good." Sasha stated flatly averting our eyes.

"Leave it alone, Joi, she'll be alright." I tried to play the mediator and comforter at the same time.

Joi gave me a look that said give her a few more minutes and she could get some answers from her. It wasn't necessary to keep badgering the girl but Joi felt otherwise. Our idea of helping a friend was vastly different. All three of us have contrasting personalities so as we interact there will be differences. In my mind, the main objective was to help not hurt.

Since the principal put a restriction on how I could dress, I've been way more conservative with my attire, receiving way less attention. It was alright though, the star treatment was short lived. The more people notice you the more problems people will bring your way. That's not something I need in my life right now. Its hard enough just being a teenager. Beyonce, Taylor Swift, Miley Cyrus all thrive in the spotlight, I'm hardly on that level and doubt I'll ever be.

Growing pains come with the maturing process. There's so much that we each have to learn as we move into womanhood. The issues that my mom goes through, I'm not equipped to handle. Even though Chloe is a few years older than me, I'm not even ready for the things she has to deal with. Life comes in stages and as we develop, more is added on to make us complete. Mistakes will be made along the way which was by design. There's no perfect woman walking this earth, even though some of us like to think we are.

After first period, Joi and I were heading to our next period when we saw a crowd gathered by the ladies bathroom. Normally I'd just watch from afar but Joi was as nosey as they come and had to have herself in the thick of things. The faces of those close to the scene were filled with horror as we got nearer. When a couple of students saw us their looks turned to sorrow, some even shook their heads. We wondered what had them so sad.

"Y'all back up! Clear the way for the paramedics!" A student yelled out. Evidently, the incident was too much for the schools medical staff to handle because there was a crew of medics from the nearby hospital rushing in carrying bags and a gurney. In the short time I've been at this school, I've never seen any serious accidents take place.

They rushed inside the restroom then closed the door behind them. While they attended to whomever had been hurt, idle chatter commenced in the crowd.

"Somebody needs to do something about those girls." One girl from the student society spoke out openly.

"Yeah, they think they run this place. The Principal already threatened to expelled them several times." Another commented.

"I don't know what she's waiting on. Maybe this will

open her eyes." Jalen and his partner voiced to each other.

Now I was concerned for whomever they were rescuing in there, more than five minutes had passed. I saw the door crack then open wide.

"Make way! We need room!" The lead medic barked out. The crowd parted like the Red Sea as they made their way out of the bathroom. Joi and I couldn't believe who they were carrying on the gurney as they moved swiftly by us.

"Hold on just a second, Sir." Joi stopped the medic as if he didn't have a choice. "Lemme see who that is." Joi got as close as she could then nearly lost her breath. I saw what she saw and my stomach turned. Sasha was stretched out on the gurney with her face swollen, all black and blue. She was hardly recognizable.

"What the hell happened to her?" I asked hoping I would get a logical answer that justified the condition she was in. The paramedics, of course didn't offer any information, they just continued down the hallway and out the door.

"Them girls beat her up." I was surprised to hear Jalen's voice over the rest of the crowd's chatter. He was concerned, I could tell by the look of worry on his face.

"What girls?" Joi asked with an angry scowl.

"You know, Ursula and her crew. They've been bullying other girls around here over the last year or so. I guess your friend Sasha was on the list of victims."

"But why? She doesn't bother anyone. She's an honor

roll student destined to go to college. What did she do to deserve this?" I cried out pleading with my eyes for answers. Jalen saw the tears forming but looked helpless because there was nothing he could do.

"Sharice, those girls don't care how good she is or what's in her future. They're miserable and get off on seeing others suffer, especially the weak." Jalen tried to explain.

"Sasha is not weak!" Joi defended. "She just stays to herself. Trouble was the last thing she wanted."

"Ursula is heartless and has trained her little crew to be the same. There have been rumors of other such incidents but none as serious as this. Just check out the SkoolChat site, there are postings." Jalen expressed. This was the most he had spoken to us, I just wished it was under better circumstances.

I went on the site and sure enough, the evidence was visual. I was astonished that there were videos and accounts of these bullying incidents floating around on the schools social media network yet nothing had been done about it.

"Why hasn't anyone reported Ursula to the Principal or the police for that matter?" I looked to Joi then Jalen.

"Everyone is afraid of those girls." Jalen said.

"Even the men? Why hasn't any men spoken up about this? Or are you scared too?" I challenged. It was low, sure, but we were in search of answers and I didn't have time to concern myself with feelings.

"A lot of guys say that may its not their business and

they don't get involved." He explained the men's position.

"Now that's just sad." Joi retorted. "And weak. Ursula needs to be bullying some of you guys and see how y'all handle that business." Jalen took offense.

"Let's be clear, ain't no girl gonna be handling me any old kinda way."

"So why is it OK for it to happen to Sasha? Someone who is innocent. Who is really equipped to defend themselves when they're being bullied or ganged up on? From the looks of her, its obvious that's what happened."

"Well, its my business now." Jalen suddenly had a change of heart.

"Why now, Jalen?"

"Because before it really wasn't close to home but I see how it is affecting you. And what affects you, affects me."

What Jalen said made me smile. Joi noticed our connection and diverted her attention to him.

"Jalen, does that go for me too?" I couldn't believe she would stoop to flirting openly in front of me.

"What?" Jalen was just as taken aback as I was. She didn't hesitate to repeat herself.

"Do I affect you?" She had some nerve. Here it was our closest friend had just been abused and she was standing here boldly making a play for my man. Well, OK, he's not my man yet, but she knew the deal. And she was crossing the line.

"Hey y'all, I'll get with you later." Jalen took that

opportunity to escape an awkward situation. As soon as he was out of earshot, I lit into Joi.

"How dare you, Joi?" I gave her a menacing stare.

"What, Reecie? I saw the way he was looking at me, so I hollered." I was instantly hurt by her total disregard for our boundaries. Joi had to be delusional to think that Jalen wanted her over me. He was standing there facing me, talking to me the whole time. She was the one who noticed him flirting with me from the beginning. Sasha warned me to keep my eye on him because there were girls watching, I didn't know the main one was Joi. I wish Sash was here to witness this. Hell, I just wish she was here.

"But you knew I was interested in Jalen, right?" I said in a soft tone, hoping to appeal to her friendship. Maybe she would see how she just hurt me.

"All I saw was you two exchanging looks like some sort of puppy love. I didn't think it was anything special." Her nonchalance showed me her true colors.

"Damn, Joi, that's wrong as hell." I said as I walked away towards my next class. If I could go any further away from her I would.

The rest of the day my mind was teetering back and forth from Sasha's condition to Joi trying to intercept my man. My emotions were so in conflict with each other, it was hard to tell if I was coming or going. The bell rang ending the days classes and it couldn't have come soon enough. With all that had transpired it seemed like two days rolled into one.

When I closed my locker door, Joi was standing

there waiting for me. She didn't say anything and neither did I. We were supposed to be friends, in my mind there were certain codes that friends don't break, she violated. My mom always spoke about forgiveness and how even your enemies need to be prayed for, I didn't understand it when she said it, now I'm finding it even harder to conceive. Joi wasn't my enemy, that I was sure of. We never know what motivates people to do what they do. It just shows that nothing can be for certain. The world was cruel and full of surprises. From one moment to the next, things could change. I see that life was unpredictable.

I walked off from Joi but she chose to follow, trying to finally explain herself. We got outside in front of the school, the place where the three of us used to meet. It was just some hours ago that we were all together ready to start our day. If we only knew that by the close of the day one of us would be in the hospital, we'd try our best to change the outcome.

I stood by the school zone sign where I waited for my dad to pick me up. Joi came up and stood beside me.

"Reecie, please talk to me. We've been friends way too long for us to be mad at each other over a boy." Joi attempted to make the situation seem like it was minor.

"I thought we were better than that too, but I guess I had you all wrong. I don't know you as well as I thought."

"I am the same friend I've always been, Reecie." Now it was her turn to plead for forgiveness.

Before I could even respond to her, a van pulled to a

screeching hault in front of us, startling both Joi and I. Two men dressed in all black jumped out, each grabbing one of us and tossing our lightweight bodies into the vehicle. Hoods were placed over our heads and then everything went black.

CHAPTER SEVENTEEN

Cookie

"SANDRA, DID YOU PICK REECIE UP FROM SCHOOL?" I cringed when I saw Carl's name light up on my screen. I know it was wrong but lately I've found it hard to be in a good space with him.

"Carl, of course not, I dropped her off. You're the one whose supposed to pick her up in the afternoon." I wondered what he was up to.

"I know. I'm here now, she's not out in front like she usually is."

"Did you check with her teachers inside, sometimes she'll have after school activities that she forgets about."

"I already did that." Carl said. "They cancelled all activities due to an incident that happened earlier today."

"Incident? Was she involved?" Now I was beginning to get concerned.

"No. A number of Reecie's friends said they saw her

and her Joi at the end of the day getting things together to leave." Carl explained. He was being thorough, asking the right questions. I was becoming agitated.

"Then where is she, Carl?" Worry was slowly setting in. My baby wasn't where she was supposed to be and that was a problem.

"I don't know but I'm gonna find out." Carl tried to reassure me.

"I sure hope so. In fact, I'm on my way."

"Sandra, you don't have to come, I'll find out what's going on." It was too late, I had already hit end on the call, grabbed my keys, and started out the door.

"Mom, Gabriel wants to take me to the movies, can I go?" Chloe asked catching me in stride. She picked a great time to ask me something, my mind was so preoccupied she could've asked me to go skydiving butt naked and I would say yes.

"Sure, Chloe, be careful." I replied and it probably shocked her. It was a school night which meant there was supposed to be no going out until the weekend.

"Where are you going in such a hurry?" Chloe asked as if she was concerned.

"Something happened with your sister. I have to run over to the school real fast. She hasn't called you, has she?"

"No mom."

"OK, just checking."

"Well, let me know if you need me" she offered.

"OK I will." I believe we both knew our words were just tossed in the wind as a formality.

I got on the road with my mind full of worry, emotionally I was in shambles. The school wasn't that far from our home but it seemed like an eternity to make it there. It was like visions of horror kept filling my thoughts about Reecie. I tried to hope for the best yet I was thinking the worst. I'm sure Carl was just as concerned as I was, she is his baby girl, too.

When I arrived at the school, Carl was parked, sitting behind the wheel with a distressed look on his face. I plopped down in the passenger seat of his car and for a minute we just sat in silence. He looked distraught and for the first time in a long time, I felt compassion for Carl. His body language was slumped, as if he had been beaten, defeated.

"What did they say?" I asked quietly.

"Sandra I probably spoke with twenty different people. I even asked the custodian if he'd seen anything, they all said they witnessed her leave. Some say she was seen in front of the school with her friend Joi."

"That's who she usually meets when I drop her off. Sasha wasn't there with them?" I asked feeling something wasn't right, a mother just knows things.

"No and I thought that was odd, the three of them were inseparable."

"What about Joi, has she been seen?"

"Same thing, she was waiting in front of the school with Sharice. Her parents are inside asking questions too."

We were totally at a loss for words, weakened and powerless by our circumstances. Then a new fear entered my mind. How were we going to break the news to Chloe, the news was still fresh to us. Our next step was to alert the police. Carl thinks we should give her a few hours to make contact with us.

"I have a friend at the department that will help us figure this out." Carl offered out of nowhere. I chose silence as my response. We were brought together by tragedy, however this doesn't solve any of our present issues, in fact, it only magnifies them. His presentation of those separation papers was still at the forefront of my mind. In light of what's on our plate at the moment, I was willing to be a team player.

"Do you think its too soon to get them involved? Maybe she and Joi went somewhere else after school, or her phone's battery was dead?" I was reaching at straws because I did have any clear answers.

"Joi's folks said they had some after school plans that had to be rescheduled. Her mom is worried sick." Carl explained.

"I'm sure she is, I am too. I'm going to head home Carl, just in case she shows up."

"I'm going to the church." I looked at him quizzically.

"For what?" I asked like that was a foreign place.

"To pray."

As I drove home, I built my hopes up to think that Reecie would be there waiting for me. We could discuss what happened, fix something to eat together then pick out her clothes like we always do. Visions of the things we do kept filtering through my mind, like her enthusiasm for dance. She loved to mimic routines she'd seen online or create new ones that would accent her rhythmic moves. It brought me pure joy to watch her do something she truly loved.

When I got home, the emptiness was haunting. Chloe was out gallivanting with Gabriel, Carl was at the church, and my baby was somewhere out there with Lord knows whom. I checked the phone for the hundredth time, then her room for any clues, nothing. Her safety was my main concern, a little girl in this huge city, there was so much that worried me. The news didn't make it any better. Accounts of people, mainly black women, were being abducted in the Washington D.C. area. It was a national crisis but it was a problem predominantly in the city. To think Sharice could be a victim of something as horrible as human trafficking.

From what I saw on the news and read in the papers, these women were collected, warehoused, and groomed for sale. The same thing was happening overseas in Libya. Brown skinned women were being tricked into other countries with hopes of a better life then enslaved, traded or sold to wealthy owners like in the old slavery days. Who knew those times would repeat over 400 years later.

These are difficult times in a corrupt world, the Bible speaks of such times. We as parents try our best to shield and protect our children from the dangers that were present. Sharice has no idea what evils lurk outside the front door. There's really nothing to prepare children for the unexpected, we just hope that the unforeseen doesn't happen. I guess we were the unlucky ones.

For me, I feel like I failed as a mom by not keeping my daughter safe. You think you have it all figured out until something happens to raise questions. Life can throw some mean curve balls, I , by no means do not excel at hitting home runs. Success, however, is measured by how well you adjust to things you are not accustomed to.

I sat and I waited, hoping for her to miraculously come through the door with her bright smile, bringing joy to my day. I went to her room again then closed the door, walking away like it was a CSI crime scene. It was hard to stay positive when it seemed like the odds were stacked up. The quiet in the house gave me time to think, too much time.

Our bedroom, the place where I used to find peace, now had a certain coldness present. As I looked around there were small reminders of happiness. Then one thing stood out that vanquished the memory, the manila envelope containing those legal papers Carl had drawn up. With all our turmoil as a couple, did we miss a sign that Sharice was being affected?

It was time to put my personal feelings aside, differences with Carl aside, even growing emotions for Adrian aside and put the focus where it belonged, with our missing daughter. My cell's ringtone snapped me back to the present time. Looking down I saw Chloe's name glowing. I wondered what she could want, knowing her it was probably something selfish.

"Yes Chloe." I answered not hiding my annoyance. I was probably wrong for that but my emotions were off kilter.

"Hey mom, any word from Reecie? Dad told me something like she wasn't at school when he went to pick her up." She was in a bubbly mood, instantly I felt a lump in my throat questioning her heart.

"No Chloe. Nothing yet."

"The strangest thing happened to us tonight." I really wasn't in the mood to entertain her story, however I listened, it may have been a welcome distraction. "Gabriel and I were riding when we noticed a car tailing us. After a few miles, Gabriel picked up their movements and came up with a plan. The car followed us all the way to this fix-it shop one of Gabriel's friends owned. The car lost sight of us as we pulled into one of the bays. Waiting for few minutes, we thought they might lose patience and leave. But they were sitting right there when we pulled out. The difference this time was we were in a different car. We sat and watched them wait until they got tired and drove off. So we followed them."

"Chloe that's dangerous." I said worried for her safety now. But she was with Gabriel and I knew how he moved from experience.

"I know mom. We're being careful."

"Do you have any idea who they were? I asked.

"No, but they lead us to an office park with storage units in there. Two more cars and a van all met in the lot."

"They didn't see you guys, did they?" They were playing a mean game, they were still teenagers in an adult world that plays for keeps.

"They were so caught up with whatever was in the van that I'm sure we were unnoticed."

"A van?" Her story was getting more intriguing by the second. "What were these people into?" I asked more for myself.

"I don't really know, mom. We saw them carry two large objects wrapped in what looked like black carpet or tarp and take them around to the back. Gabriel said there was too much going on so we left."

"Good call. No need in you guys getting involved in something illegal or maybe worse."

I already had one daughter missing, I couldn't live with myself if something were to happen to Chloe too.

"Just come home, Chloe, we need to figure out what we're going to do about your sister."

"I'm on my way. We'll figure something out together."

CHAPTER EIGHTEEN
Carl

"USUALLY, I WOULD ASK IF THERE ARE ANY PRAYER requests that need to be sent up. Usually, I would serve as a proud intercessor just as the Lord makes intercession for us. As a prayer warrior, I truly understand the power of prayer. However, today I'm in need of some prayer. My family is in search of some powerful prayer warriors. My wife and I toiled over and over whether to discuss our personal matters publicly but we decided it would be best to open up to our church family because we believe that multiple prayers produce magnificent results."

There were choruses of "Amens" that resonated across the room. Sunday service was packed to capacity with people coming out in droves renewing their commitment to fellowship. Service to the Lord outweighed the rumors, suspicions, allegations that surfaced against me. I prayed for the hearts of my faithful church family to be softened and although it took some time, they eventually came around.

"If you haven't noticed, our youngest daughter, Sharice, isn't in attendance this morning. For some God awful reason she didn't return home from school. To ensure her safety, my wife or myself would either drop her off or pick her up from school daily, even those measures weren't enough. We had the authorities put out an Amber Alert to make our community aware that she's missing. Your prayers for her speedy return to us is needed." I heard murmurs from the congregation which I anticipated with such shocking news. Sharice wasn't just our daughter, she was a daughter to many in the church who loved her spirit and genuine personality. They witnessed her dance performances and her presence at Sunday school. Sharice was definitely a fixture at the church as much as Sandra or myself.

"This has been a tough 48 hours for us. Our family has gone through a number of trials but none as trying as this. So we're asking at this time everyone join hands. Right now, as we touch and agree, we welcome in the spirit. For He says in His word that when two or three are gathered together in my name, I am there in the midst. I'm sure there are far more than two or three agreeing today that we want Sharice back home safe and sound with us."

I asked Sister Ruby to come forth and lead us in prayer. She has been with Victory in Faith since the beginning. She witnessed the baptism of many of the church children, including Sharice. As she made her way down from her place in the choir, I could see the emotion drawn all over her face. I knew this would be tough on her, however Ms. Ruby's a strong prayer warrior, probably our strongest. Whenever we're in need of a special prayer she always delivers.

As she prayed, I could hear weeping from several people in the congregation that showed the power of her words and the effect they had on others. Sister Ruby was truly gifted in prayer, definitely anointed with the Spirit of God. It made my heart warm to know it was my daughter she was praying for, she was innocent and didn't deserve whatever horrors that lurked out there. A sense of comfort came over me, which showed me what we were doing was the right thing.

In times of trouble our first inclination is to question God. Who are we to do that? Isn't he the same God who brings joy when things are going well? He says in His word that I am the same yesterday, today and forever. His word tends to get lost when we encounter difficulties, that's when we need to depend on Him most.

I felt a hand touch my shoulder as Sister Ruby was closing prayer. It was a strange touch, one that didn't feel like it was filled with the spirit. I heard gasps of breath and when I opened my eyes they nearly jumped out of my head in shock.

"You've got some nerve coming here." I whispered with as much angst as I could muster, looking at Carl Jr. in the eye.

"I have something I need to talk to you about." He told me while searching my face for acceptance.

"I don't have anything to talk to you about. You should be talking to the police."

"Why? Did you press charges against me? You really did that to me, dad?"

"Dad? Man, don't dad, me, after what you did. I gave you a chance and you stole from me." People were beginning to stir at the commotion. My irritation made my voice raise an octave drawing attention.

"Is there some where we can talk?" He kept insisting on carrying on a conversation. I really didn't want to make any more of this situation. This day was too important for my family. I obliged his request.

"OK, meet me in my office in ten minutes." Then I went to meet with Deacon Pryor and Sister Ruby. I couldn't even focus because my mind was on what this man could possibly have to say.

In my office, Carl Jr. was waiting there patiently with a sheepish look on his face. I hope he wasn't doing that to gain sympathy from me because I wasn't buying it. Without a word I went in and he followed. I thought this should be interesting.

"Have a seat," I told him as I sat behind my desk.

"There's something you should know about that situation." He started.

"What?"

"You have a thief in your church, but its not me." I couldn't believe what I was hearing.

"What are you talking about? There are people who saw you."

"Yes, people saw me working and assumed that when

the money was gone, they figured two and two equaled four."

"Well, if it were up to my calculations, the math adds up." I said sarcastically but really meant it.

"I knew once the news got back to you, all the fingers would point at me."

"And why wouldn't they be? Where else would they point?"

"What if I told you I know where your money is?" My eyes lit up now totally interested in what he had to say.

"Are you playing with me?"

"At this point, I'm trying to clear my name the best I can, so no, I'm not playing with you. See, what everybody doesn't know is that the money never left the room."

"Huh? I don't get it. The report came to me that you left with the offering drop." I explained.

"Not true. Yes, I did leave but after the offering drop was left unattended."

"I don't understand." I was totally confused at his tale.

"The satchel that contained the drop was still in the room, sitting on the table. I guess whoever was supposed to put it up didn't show. I was in the bathroom working when I saw the bag."

"So what did you do?"

"I had a choice to make, I could do the right thing or the wrong thing, I chose the right thing. I came out of the bathroom, saw that no one was around, waited a minute for someone to come in then I put it up."

"You put it up?" I was in disbelief.

"Yup." He was really sure of his self.

"The drop bag?" I has to be for sure.

"Yes Sir." A sense of relief engulfed me on all fronts. In a split moment I went from angry to elated.

"Can I ask you where?"

"I'd rather show you, but dad when I show you where your money is, I need you to do something for me." At that point, i was ready to concede to anything.

"What do you want? Some money? I'm willing to pay you a small reward if that's what you're speaking of." I knew there was a catch, it was OK though, everyone had an angle.

"Actually no, that's not what I was referring to. I just want an apology and a ticket out of town."

"Wait a minute. I don't understand. You're not guilty and you want to leave?" I was kind of thrown off by his wishes.

"Definitely. You see, just a few minutes ago you thought I made off with your precious church money, wanted me arrested and everything without a chance to defend myself. So, why should I stick around. All I wanted was a relationship with you and your family, but I see that may not be possible."

There was nothing I could say because he was absolutely right. I never gave him a chance or the benefit of the doubt for that matter. He head every right to be mad and want to leave town, we never made him feel welcome. I've been so focused on trying to salvage my family, I had a family member in my face and didn't even recognize him as family until it was too late.

Without another word on my part I followed Carl Jr. to the collection drop room. He took me to a place in the room that I didn't know existed, inside a small compartment, Carl pulled out a dust covered drop satchel with its contents still intact. I had to admit, I was totally surprised at his honesty and embarrassed to the fullest. The way he looked at me dug a pit in my stomach and dropped a hot coal in it.

He gave me this expressionless stare then turned and walked out before I could give him his well deserved apology. The man did the most honorable thing, be honest when all the odds were against him. I overlooked my own staff who was obviously negligent and accused an innocent man. Jesus was in the same position, an innocent man persecuted and found guilty for no wrongdoing. I am just as guilty for not hearing him out. I may have found the missing church money but was it worth losing a son? I may never know.

CHAPTER NINETEEN

Adrian

IT WAS GETTING HARD TO HOLD BACK MY EXCITEMENT, almost as hard as keeping the news that I was going home from the nosey dudes in here. I had one more day behind the walls, one more wake up, and one more opportunity to rest and get my thoughts together before I enter the real world. The mindset of the incarcerated was always moment to moment. On the outside, my way of thinking had to change.

I decided not to go back to detail, I figured what's the use, Pam and I weren't seeing eye to eye. Truthfully, I didn't know how to react when she told me she was pregnant with my seed. I guess I didn't give her the response she expected because the few days following the news her mood was rather snooty. It was evident in how she treated me, which I could deal with but the other inmates witnessed her mood swing and that wasn't a good look, not something I wanted to get caught up in.

Besides, there was no real need for me to work with me being so close to the end. At first, I said I would help train the next orderly who was to be hired, then I decided not to subject myself to the "Pam treatment". So when they called for me, I just told them I wasn't going. Now in prison, you can get in trouble for not reporting to a detail, but I was on my way out the door, what could they do to me, really.

In the midst of all the dorm chatter, I sat on my bunk, out of the way with my mind elsewhere. There was so much I had to do by tomorrow. Within a few days I needed to find a job, get my driver's license, set up a bank account, buy some clothes, and above all things take a hot bath. After years of taking showers it would be pleasant change to sit in a tub of hot water.

The first thing on my agenda was to talk to my brother to see when he was coming to pick me up. I wasn't trying to give these folks one second more than I have to. He was due to be here bright and early with a change of clothing, ready to take me to report to my parole officer. The whole transition back into society will be challenging, having a good relationship with my P.O. would be a wonderful start.

"Addison, what's up?" I greeted when he answered on the second ring.

"What's good, lil bro?" His voice didn't have its usual zest, maybe his excitement for me coming home had him exhausted as did me.

"Nothing much, just making sure everything's all set for tomorrow. When should I look for you?" There was hesitation in his tone which didn't sound reassuring.

"Ahhh..I'll be there sometime in the morning."

"Bro, what's up? Is there something you need to tell me?" A lump formed in my throat and I had an eerie feeling coming upon me.

"Look, I'll tell you when I come to pick you up, bro." Then he hung up abruptly.

What did he mean by that? I was left with a host of unanswered questions. My brother was acting weird but I was in a position of need. Getting out with nothing automatically makes me a dependent. Not really how I wanted to start but I didn't have much of a choice.

Over the years, I've had family members distance themselves from me claiming my situation shed a bad light on them. Early on it had bothered me, however as time passed I got used to the disappointments. Diminishing visits and broken promises became the norm after while, I just developed a shell and became numb to it.

Its hard to maintain mental stability being locked away. Between outside issues with family and the oppressive position prison administration takes, its enough to drive a person crazy. If the outside world only knew how the treatment was inside some of the jails and prison facilities, they would scream injustice. The problem that exists, many of the officials keep a hushed mouth to the dealings inside.

Just last month we had an incident that almost got volatile and ended up going public. One of the worst things prisons can do was to violate an inmates rights.

Even though we're incarcerated, we are still human beings and we still have rights. Something as simple as eating a meal was often taken for granted by staff members. Evidently they had been getting away with violating those basic rights, but that soon came to an end.

In the feeding area known as the "chowhall", the food preparers for the prison had the audacity to give us a meal that was less than adequate. Malcolm Sharpe, a politically motivated inmate, noticed it first and mentioned it to one of the officers on duty in the chowhall. The tray that they served didn't have the proper amount of food on it, even worse the main course, oven fried chicken, was missing.

We only got chicken once a month so people looked forward to that day. When Malcolm said something to the food service manager, Ms. Hankerson, she simply remarked, "We ran out of chicken so this is all we're serving." People in line behind Malcolm heard her response to his complaint and became outraged. Now Malcolm, who was usually a peaceful man, couldn't believe her insensitivity. He was not one to stand down in the face of injustice.

Malcolm Sharpe was a middle aged man born in the late 60s from parents who were entangled in the struggle. Even though his demeanor was considered docile on the surface, his radical genes were deeply rooted and were ready to rear their ugly head. Out of his fifty years on this earth, 23 of them had been spent begin the walls of various penitentiaries. He had been transferred several times because he wasn't afraid to challenge the system with grievances. That 50 year old man was feared from institution to institution. He had had enough and hunger was his motivation to initiate action.

"Ain't no way this is all you're serving us. We are entitled to eat what everybody else is eating. They are eating chicken." He waved his hand over the entire chowhall. "So we want chicken."

"Sir, you need to step away from the serving window" the security officer ordered.

"I'm not stepping away from nothing. What they need to do is find us some food." Malcolm ordered back.

"Yeah," someone shouted from the line as a crowd started to form at the window. The officer saw the mob and got worried.

"Disperse! Right now!" He tried to regain control but it was too late. Everyone had joined the protest, it only took one to set it off, Jada Pinkett style. The service crew and manager had closed the window fearing the worst.

"Maybe you're not familiar with me," Malcolm said to the guard in a calm voice. "I'm Malcolm Sharpe with an "E", after today you will know."

"Officer Elam, in need of back up in true chow hall!" He shouted into his radio that was clipped to his shoulder. Within a minute there were five of the Goon Squad members along with ten other officers. Four of them were women, why they sent them, who knew. This was a potentially dangerous situation in need of force.

The crowd saw what I saw and slowly move back.

Our numbers were greater than theirs yet psychologically they seemed to have the control.

"Do not panic and do not show fear!" Malcolm spoke to his compatriots. "They can't do anything to us if we do not pose a threat."

"The hell if we can't do anything. You, Mr. Sharpe, are a threat. We did our homework on you. From camp to camp you have a history of creating disturbances, well not at our camp. Lofton will not stand for it." One of the black suited men announced. Then he pulls out a stick with a lighted tip. The other four followed his lead and armed themselves with their tasers.

Malcolm laughed as they swayed side to side waiting to make a move. He wasn't going to engage, instead he would just watch. Over the years, Malcolm trained for combat situations such as this. He studied different defense styles and how to deal with multiple assailants, he excelled in that. He worked out hard, stayed in tip top shape in the event war ever broke out. Well, the way he saw it, this was the closest thing to war.

"You guys might want to put those sticks down before someone gets hurt." Malcolm said calmly as if he was in full control. One of the guards looked antsy, itching to make move but he had to get the OK from his supervisor.

"The only one who's gonna get hurt is you if you don't get on the wall and put your hands behind your back." Malcolm was amused at this cat and mouse game with the guys. He could tell who had been trained and who haven't.

"Yeah, put your hands up!" Another guard chimed in as he inched closer to Malcolm with his taser stick close to his side.

"You mean like this?" Malcolm took a step towards the guard then in a quick motion, he shot the guard a hard punch to his sternum followed by an elbow across his chin causing him to double over in pain. One of the other goons rushed in without warning while his team stood watching in astonishment. That move was to Malcolm's delight, an opponent's aggressiveness worked to his advantage. The man came at Malcolm swinging wildly. It didn't take much to avoid the contact of the other taser.

Malcolm weaved the uncontrolled swipe then used his momentum to catch him off balance with a hip toss. The man was probably twice Malcolm's weight but his knowledge of leverage and weight transfer that was taught by his sensei, he was able to operate the maneuver perfectly. The goon landed squarely on his back with a thud, howling in agony.

The one thing these guys weren't prepared for was a confrontation with a skilled man. There's no simulation for live combat and Malcolm was making the most of their inexperience. Some of the security team haven't been on their job as long as Malcolm has been trained. Their lack of training proved to be costly.

With two of the so called toughest men at the institution on the floor, the others felt as if their pride and reputation was on the line. Two came at Malcolm at the same time thinking that the numbers would increase their odds. Not knowing how to attack him also became their weakness.

He sized up the two with a quick glance then watched to see which one was the aggressor by how they chose to attack. They didn't come at the same time, one was slightly in front of the other which made it easier for Malcolm to counter. Like a fool, the first man rushed at him hoping to wrap him up in a bear hug. The move was very predictable and he anticipated it with a stiff front kick to his assailant's knee. He immediately went down in searing pain holding his knee that was visibly out of place. Malcolm side stepped the tumbling guard, readying himself for his next move which was a spinning back fist to the other guard's open face. He rushed in head first right in the perfect position to receive the strike. His bloodied lip made him retreat. Malcolm knew that continuing this would be futile. There was more of them and he wasn't in a Jet Li movie, eventually they would outnumber him. He had done enough damage to their security team and his reputation would be forever cemented in history but what point would it make if justice wasn't served.

Malcolm with his hands raised, surrendered to the remainder of the authority figures who stood in shock at what just happened.

"Please put your hands behind your back, so we can cuff you. We are not going to hurt you, Mr. Sharpe." Captain Rogers spoke respectfully. This woman was usually as nasty as they come, she had no regard for inmates. I guess after she saw where Malcolm Sharpe had no regard for the welfare of her security team, she changed her approach to a more mild one. She may have been afraid of suffering the same fate as them because this man was obviously dangerous.

"I'm not cuffing up until these people get the proper food they deserve." He said in protest. Captain stood at a safe distance contemplating his request. It was like he was holding all the cards.

"We'll get them fed, Sir." She replied.

"No. Not just fed. Give them chicken like everyone else." At that moment the director of food service came out to address the protestors with an announcement.

"Everyone please have a seat. We are back there preparing chicken breast patties fresh out of the box. We just got these in, the other inmates haven't even had these." He advertised in excitement. He seemed proud of himself like he had done a great deed. If his staff would've prepared the right amount the first time we would have been in that position.

"There you go, Mr. Sharpe, you heard it, now we're gonna have to escort you to the hole." Malcolm gave a calming nod to the waiting crowd, as we sat down and got ready to eat. We all secretly wondered what would happen to Malcolm after that. He complied by allowing them to put the handcuffs on him, then he and the hobbling, injured officers left.

That day was something to be remembered. It showed me that we are considered less than human by prison staffers and if we don't stand up for our basic human rights they would continue to enslave us.

I didn't realize I had drifted off to sleep until I heard someone calling my name repeatedly.

"Adrian! Yo, Adrian! Damn yo ass sleeping hard," I woke up to see Richie Rich standing over me. I was startled a bit but quickly came to my senses. "They've been calling you over the intercom." He said.

"12 on the floor! 12 on the floor!" Someone hollered out for all to hear and to get on point.

"Oh relax y'all, I ain't here to stir up nothing", the young officer coolly strolled in and remarked. Officer Burke was one of the most laid back guys you ever wanted to meet, he was proof that all staff wasn't bad.

"Upshaw, you not ready yet? You got to pack it up." He said completely catching me off guard.

"Huh....what time is it, officer?" I must've been out of it.

"Man, its almost 8 o'clock." Rich answered. "Where you going, brah?"

"He's going home." Burke announced with excitement like it was his release. I really didn't want it broadcasted like that.

"Home? Damn, homie, you weren't gonna tell anybody? Hey y'all, our boy A.U. is trying to sneak out on us." That's when nearly the whole dorm made their way over to my bunk to see what the commotion was about. I had seen guys I've never said a word to coming to wish me well.

"Y'all give him some space and let him pack his stuff." The officer said. A few of the fellas gave me a hard time but for, the most part they were all happy for me. "Your folks will be here to get you after count.

"Thanks Burke." He watched like it was his first time seeing someone going home. He hadn't been at the camp long so he was going to witness many 'firsts'. For me, I'm on my 'lasts' as far as the system goes. Last meal was yesterday, last wake up was a few minutes ago, now it was time to say my last goodbyes.

As I looked at these familiar faces standing around me, some had joy in their eyes others looked as if they were envious of the opportunity to get away from the underworld we had made our home. I never referred to prison as my home. Home is where the heart is and my heart was never here. I always knew I'd get a second chance at life on the outside, my fear was what I'd do with the new opportunity.

The faces I had become accustomed to waking up to every morning watched me gather my things. Anything I didn't plan on taking, I gave away to those dear to me. JoJo, Clepto, Richie Rich, B-Smooth were all there like they've always been. The only one who wasn't there from the original crew was Preacher Man. I was gonna miss my guys, probably Preach the most. He introduced me to church and that's where I met up with God, making Him a very important part of my life. I also met Sandra there and she became equally as important to my life as going to church.

Continuing on a positive spiritual path was what I needed to focus on. Rebirthing my faith, reviving my life, and reuniting my family were the most important goals I wanted to tackle, in that order. Seeing where things would go with Cookie had me intrigued as well. There would be obstacles when it came to her situation, so I would tread lightly.

I had much to sort out, much to take in, after so many years away. I gave Rich my phone and told him I'd be in touch. In the back of my mind I knew I wouldn't. I was moving forward, old things left behind. They would understand, real men always understand. I was real with them and they kept it real with me. I'll never forget that......or them for that matter.

CHAPTER TWENTY

The Watchers

THEY WERE GETTING TIRED OF HOLDING THE LITTLE Andrews' girl hostage. After they ditched the other girl, Joi Holmes, they moved forward with their plan. The problem came when young Rico felt like he was being treated like a babysitter. His job was simple, just keep the girl restrained and don't let his identity be revealed. He ended up failing at both.

Rico was playing Madden on the PlayStation when Reecie kept disturbing his entertainment groove.

"Hey...hey boy," she called out from a corner where she was moved to. Her hands and feet were still bound but they took her gag and hood off fearing any potential dangers. They weren't trying to hurt the little girl especially by accident.

"Hey boy!" Rico was doing his best to ignore her but couldn't take it anymore.

"Who in the hell are you calling boy?" He snapped at

her. She just giggled knowing that she had struck a nerve. By observing his actions, Reecie could tell Rico was the youngest one who frequented the warehouse, storage type place she was being kept in. She was glad they took the hood off so she could get her bearings.

"You. I want some water." She demanded

"Some water? Get up and get it yourself." Rico burst out laughing like that was the funniest thing he had heard.

"Real funny. You won't be laughing so hard when you guys get caught by the police."

"Who gonna call them? You? Your preacher daddy?"

"When my dad gets a hold of you, you're gonna wish you never touched me." Reecie threatened.

"And I should be scared? What's he gonna do, bible thump me to death? I don't think I have much to worry about."

"You'll see. She responded confidently. "So what's up with the water?" Rico went back to ignoring her, focusing back on his game. She just blew out some air in disgust, obviously annoyed by him.

He wasn't going to make the same mistake twice. He and Demani were transporting the girls from the storage unit facility to a van. Pappo was always a step ahead, like a skilled chess player. He told the two nephews to take the girls to another location. While walking them to the vehicle, Reecie complained of the blindfold being too tight around her eyes. She continued to shriek in pain until they got into the van. Rico felt a sense of guilt because he tied them up and remembered Pappo saying not to hurt them in any way.

Against his better judgement, he loosened the restraint around her eyes, trying to retie it so it wouldn't be so tight. The sash slipped out of his fingers and into her lap. He did his best to gather it up quickly but not before they locked eyes. Reecie had seen him and he knew he had messed up thoroughly. She made no secret of the incident for the sole purpose of exposing Rico's incompetence to his cousin, Demani.

It was decided to rid themselves of the other little girl, Joi, and concentrate all efforts on Reecie. Pappo had a plan to negotiate with the Andrews family. He didn't want to harm her, all he wanted was the money she stole from him. He could've aggressively went after Gabriel but he knew that apprehending the daughter of the famed Pastor would give him more leverage, make his chances better of retrieving his money.

The nephew's sloppiness was compounded by not noticing a bystander and that fell on the shoulders of Demani. Pappo held him more responsible because of his age. When he asked if they were seen by any one he said he didn't think so, but Rico spilled the beans hoping to get the weight off of him. Rico saw a man who appeared to be cleaning out his storage unit, like he was going somewhere. It could've been nothing but to Pappo nothing was something.

Pappo made a promise to his nephew Richie Rich that he would do everything in his power to help him get out. When the therapist, Maxine Stinson, got jailed for perjuring herself it was a slight setback but he felt confident she would cooperate with the right amount of pressure. Now that she's out of jail there was still hope. In his mind, he would get her to concede to his wishes. Where there was a will there's a way.

Richard Crawford's case was continued until another date was scheduled. He sat at Lofton State Prison, awaiting transport back for court. His only hope was that his uncle could convince Maxine to somehow issue another statement. It may be a long shot but what else did he have. Pappo knew the judge wouldn't give her that chance again, once you have the opportunity to tell the truth and you lie, who will believe you after that. He didn't want to tell Richie that, he didn't want to dampen his spirits. Pappo had another plan up his sleeve but the most important thing was collecting the stolen money.

CHAPTER TWENTY-ONE
Cookie

I DECIDED TO CANCEL ALL MY APPOINTMENTS FOR THE day. Although I needed the money, that was hardly as important as needing my daughter home with me. I could only imagine what Reecie might be going through being away from us like this. She has never been separated from us any longer than an occasional sleepover with a friend. That wasn't but a night or two, nothing like these circumstances.

Carl and I have been worried sick about her. So much so that we agreed to put aside our differences for the moment and focus on the safety of our daughter. One thing I was sure of, Reecie meant everything to Carl as she did to me. I witnessed him breaking down daily and I could tell the whole disappearance was wearing on him. The hardest part was not knowing. The police didn't have any leads so there were no updates to give us, no matter how many times we called. That alone was frustrating.

With so much going on at home I almost forgot that Maxine had her hearing in court tomorrow. If she wouldn't have called to remind me, I surely would've missed it.

"Believe me, Cookie, I totally understand if you don't want to come with me to court," Max had already made an excuse for me.

"No way, Max. We're friends and I want to be there for you. Who else has been riding with you through this?"

"I get it, but being a friend also means recognizing the concerns of others and I know you guys are going through a lot as a family."

"We are. But what you're dealing with is important too, plus I'm here to see it to the end. There's no way I'd leave you now." I heard her sniffling through the phone. "What's wrong, Max?" I asked worried that there may be something else.

"There's so many emotions running through me right now, some for you, the rest for me."

"I sense that you're scared." I could tell.

"I am, a little.....OK, a lot actually. I don't know what may come out of this. My son says I have nothing to worry about but I don't see how he can be so confident with my life on the line."

"I may not know what your son knows but I do know that God is working behind the scenes on your behalf. He could be working through your brother to get you to your destination."

"I sure hope so."

"Hope is the door to belief. Its time to walk in that belief. Things will turn out differently when you start to think differently." I was trying to give Max a little inspiration, some was for me too.

"Thank you, Cookie. I wish I had the spiritual strength you have."

"You do have it, Max. Its inside you, you just have to go down deep and pull it out. Do you have a bible?"

"Huh?"

"A bible, do you have one?" I could tell she was searching, not just for a Bible but for meaning too.

"Yeah, ahh let me see. OK here it is."

"Max, when was the last time you've read it?"

"I pull it out from time to time when I need it"

"You don't think this is a time of need? So, pull it out, let me show you something." I said without a second rebuttal from her.

"Aright, Cookie, but just so you know, I need a miracle."

"What you need is for God to fight your battle for you. I include myself in this, try to handle our problems ourselves." I confessed.

"What are we supposed to do?" She asked with a child like mind. She was indeed a babe in Christ.

"We're supposed to give it to God." I answered with confidence.

"What you mean? Just sit back and do nothing? I don't think that's how its supposed to work."

"You have your Bible with you yet?" I intended to show her how it works.

"I have it."

I told her to turn to Exodus where I could let her read about the story of Moses. Not the typical Ten Commandments, but the one where God works through Moses to fight the battle between the Israelites and the Amalekites. Exodus 17 describes Gods power in action when he uses the example of Moses on the hill.

God told Moses to keep his staff raised to the sky and He will make sure the Israelites keep winning. If his arms fall, then the Amalekites will start winning the battle. Moses did all he could to keep his hands up but he became tired, so his faithful friends came to his aid and held his arms up through the night. With Gods help the Israelites won the battle. The lesson I wanted to show her was as long as she kept her hands to the sky and praised God then the battle will be taken over by God.

"So, you preaching to me now, Cookie, or is this Sandra, the First Lady?" She joked.

"Actually Max, I'm preaching to myself too. You see, there are battles in my life that I can't win on my own. I've been too stubborn to let God handle things. To put it bluntly, I haven't practiced what I've been preaching.

"Cookie, I can admit, I should've been taking my spiritual life more serious. Since meeting you, I've watched how you always keep God in the equation."

"As I should, but that doesn't mean I always do the right thing." We both had to chuckle at that one.

"Nobody's perfect."

"Very true. However, I know there are things I need to improve on and I should've consulted with God before acting on my own."

"Are you referring to the situation with this Adrian fellow?" She must've been reading my thoughts.

"Him as well as other things in my life I'm not proud of."

"Well, from what you've told me about Adrian and how he makes you happy, I say follow your heart. Life is short and nothing is promised, not even tomorrow."

"Exactly, that's why I'm trying to get your mind in the right place. You never know what tomorrow may bring."

My phone lit up with an unknown number so I ended the conversation with Max reassuring her that I'd be there bright and early in the morning. I answered the other line with my thoughts still clouded, the caller quickly shocked me back into reality.

"Sandra, I have some information for you that I think you might find important." Whomever it was greeted me as if we knew each other.

"Who is this calling?" I asked hoping it wasn't a prank.

"I have no beef with you, only with your husband." He continued.

"And you said your name was again?"

"Carl."

"Carl Jr.?"

"Yes, but I don't even know if I want to claim being a junior after how he treated me, like I wasn't even his son. But that's another story."

"So what's this information you said you have?" I was interested in what news he had.

"I heard about your daughter while I was over at the church and my thoughts and prayers go out to you."

"Thank you, Carl, that really means a lot."

"Well, I was at my storage unit cleaning it out."

"You going somewhere?" All this was news to me.

"Yup. Anyway, it's what I saw that raised my eyebrows."

"What?" The suspense had me curious.

"There were these two men standing by this all black van. Two more guys came from inside, each escorting two young girls who appeared to be blindfolded and gagged." Oh my God! I couldn't believe what I was hearing. Could this be true? The police didn't have any solid leads and here it was someone we knew had what we needed. God is good.

"Carl, do you know what this means?" My thoughts were going a mile a minute.

"Now, Sandra, hold on. I don't know for sure whether that was Reecie or not. And it didn't really register until after they pulled off but I have to be honest, the whole scene looked suspicious." My spirits went down a bit when he said that. I had high hopes thinking new were close to bringing our baby home.

"So where do we go from here? How do we find her?" I was on the verge of panicking all over again.

"I don't know. I can show you where my unit is, after that I don't know what would be next.

※

I sat in the courtroom, one row behind Maxine and her lawyer, Paula Bonds. It wasn't as crowded as I thought it would be, in fact there were less people in there than the first time she went before this judge. That didn't stop the flow of people trickling in to witness judgement or injustice depending which side of the coin you were on.

There sitting on the other side of Max was a young man in a dark colored suit, bald head shining off of the ceiling lights. I remembered her mentioning her son but this man look more like a member of the Dream Team than her baby boy.

"OK, everyone can be seated. We are ready to start our proceedings for this morning." The grey haired woman voiced through her microphone, perched high on her judges seat. The way she allowed her eyeglasses to slide to the bridge of her nose made her look distinct, that's what made me remember her from before.

"Ms. Stinson, I hope you understand the serious nature of your offense. Mrs. Bonds please tell me you have something convincing to keep your client from going to jail. You do know that is the penalty, Ms. Stinson? You can go to jail if I find you guilty." She looked squarely in Max's direction with a sinister glare. I could see Max just nod.

"Your honor, we are fully aware of the ramifications of my clients actions. I have evidence I wish to present that I think will exonerate Ms. Stinson from her charge of perjury." Mrs. Bonds walked confidently towards the bench. Her short, auburn colored hairstyle gave her a strong sense of professionalism. Torry, Max's son, leaned over and whispered something in her ear. Paula Bonds spoke again. "Your honor, I've subpoenaed a witness but they haven't shown up yet."

"Well the only thing I can do is issue an warrant but in the meantime, do you have anything else to present?" She looked back at Torry and then to the door when it swung open.

"Here he is, your honor." Paula said pointing at the man walking down the aisle. Demani Crawford was being escorted by two burly bailiffs and it was obvious he wasn't happy about being there.

"Ah, Mr. Crawford, if I knew it was you we would've rolled out the red carpet for your grand entrance." The judge chided him sarcastically. There was history between the two that seemed to annoy Demani. He was walked straight to the witness stand for questioning. Immediately, Paula attacked him with a series of inquiries.

"Mr. Crawford, have you seen this woman before?" She pointed over to Maxine.

He took a good look then a deep breath. "No, I've never seen her a day in my life." When he spoke his gold capped teeth glistened. Another older gentleman came in and took a seat in the back of the courtroom.

"Now that's funny because we have audio evidence of you making calls to not only my client but to her son over there also." He didn't have a response. So the judge responded instead.

"I'd like to hear this evidence." She summoned Paula to her. She gladly went up to her with a zip lock bag containing a cellphone. The judge took it out. "Play it for me, please." She requested. Paula called Torry over to operate the phone since it was his evidence he brought. He pulled up the audio feed and the judge pressed play.

"Torry Stinson, you don't know me but I sure know you. Tell your mother, that psycho bitch, we want our 50 grand we gave her since she couldn't keep her end of the bargain."

"Who is this?"

"That's not important. What you need to concerned with is convincing your mom to come clean with those stacks. The same way I found you, I can get to her. You think you can keep her safe all the way on the West Coast? I'm sitting right down the street from her office, what can you do?"

"If you even touch her-------"

"Get my money!"

That call ended. Torry went to another file that was downloaded to his phone. He swiped a couple times then hit the screen and a conversation involving Demani and another gentleman. This time the callers were in a detailed discourse about Maxine and what they had planned for her. I was impressed by his use of technology but was completely drawn to what was being said.

"Look, uncle, I'm doing my best to get that bitch to fork over that money. I even went after her son, hoping she would bite."

"Demani, its safe to say that she has long spent the money. What person you know holds onto $50,000 that she never expected to get. You see how eager she was to receive it."

"So what's your plan?"

"If she's not willing to cooperate, we'll have to do what we have to do. I'll give you the word on how to dispose of her. Right now, there's some unfinished business I have with her friend, the First Lady."

"Are you gonna give her daughter back?"

"I will, when she returns what she stole from me."

My mouth fell open in shock. Now I knew for sure who had my baby and I was furious.

"Where is she!?" I shouted out before I knew it. "Where is she dammit!" I yelled in direction of the stand where the witness was still seated. The judge must've thought I was shooting at her.

"Excuse me, ma'am. We will have order in my courtroom. No more out bursts like that. Now who are you and how are you related to this case?"

"My name is Sandra Andrews, I'm the First Lady he referred to on that phone recording. They have my daughter."

CHAPTER TWENTY-TWO

Cookie

"Calm down, Sandra, just calm down. I can't understand what you're saying. What's this about Reecie? Who has her?" I tried to explain to Carl what I heard but was out of breath. The whole situation was too much to take in, it was all coming at me so fast. The judge was astonished at the revelations she heard. What started out as a simple perjury hearing turned into a key clue to a missing persons case.

In the back of my mind, I saw the truth slowly being revealed. Everything that I had done in the dark was coming to the light.

"Its a long, long story, Carl. I'll tell you everything when I get home."

"What you mean? When can we get Sharice back?" He sounded frantic and I didn't blame him.

"Tell Chloe to contact Gabriel."

"Huh? Gabriel? That boy she's been talking to?

Sandra, what's going on?" I knew he was lost but he would have to trust me, I would explain all out it.

"I'll see you in a few." Then I hung up before he could get another word in.

The drive home was hard. I wondered how Carl was going to react to what I was about to tell him. The past few months have been one big blur, and one secret after another. In a marriage, you think you know your mate. The things Carl had in the closet surely came as a surprise to me. From the episode with the man named Patrick who totally embarrassed Carl in public, to the pop-up visit at the church from Carl Jr. His recent past was hardly squeaky clean.

But of late, I've been pretty messy, with enough skeletons in my closet to start a museum. Going that caper with Gabriel, which ended with him getting shot, probably took the cake. It definitely wasn't befitting of a First Lady. Stolen money, tailing gangsters, shootouts. Hearing it aloud one would think it was a scene from one of those hood movies. I wasn't proud to say that I lived that caper not too long ago. I was hoping it would be a thing of the past, something that would fade away, yet here it was front and center.

Now the money embezzlement from the church was something I chose to keep secret. The funds were replaced and as long as Sister Allen stays solid then there's no need to disclose that matter. Besides, I had bigger fish to fry. Carl was going to have a hard time dealing with the fact that his wife and matriarch of his beloved church, was capable of such life threatening acts. I felt like I had to in the moment, for a friend, a good friend. Maxine deserved my best and she deserved the risk. Now putting our daughter in harms way wasn't part of the plan and I'm deeply regretful for that. Other than that detail, would I do it again? If the circumstances called for it, I'd have to say yes.

"You did what?" Carl shouted, totally taken aback by what I had just told him. "What in the hell were you thinking taking on those gangsters like that? Don't you know you could've gotten yourself hurt or even killed. Lord knows you weren't always a saint but the streets have changed drastically since you were out there."

I sure appreciated him exposing my business in front of company. Maxine and Gabriel were present.

"And did you ask for him?" He looked sternly at Gabriel as if he wasn't welcome.

"Well, yes. He was with me when all this started, when we got the money." I said feeling ashamed that I had involved so many people. I knew more questions would follow.

"This just keeps getting better and better. I thought you were just following those thugs, what's this about money?" I had to go ahead and tell him the rest before it got any deeper, he had a right to know.

"When I saw that they were handling a large quantity of money, it could help fix a problem." I saw his wheels trying to process.

"Go ahead, Sandra continue." I felt like I was in the middle of a full scale interrogation in our living room. "What kind of problem did you have that required you to rob somebody. Wow, that didn't even sound right coming out of my mouth, my wife, the mother of my kids, a robber." He mumbled under his breath.

"I had to bond my friend, Max out of jail." I said as if it were as common as going to the mailbox.

"And I take it that you're Max?" He looked towards her. She nodded awkwardly at him then smiled. "So you're the reason she's in this mess."

Maxine really didn't know what to say. I told her how Carl could be and now she is seeing it first hand. For the record, I made my own choices, nothing was forced by Max at all. In truth, it all started with me extending a helping hand. It just got deeper. She was a friend in need and I'd always been taught that friends do for friends. I haven't had many since being married so I valued Max and our relationship. Even though it started out professional, we grew as we shared our truths.

"Carl, Max didn't know the mess she was getting into until it was too late. I made my own choice to help her." I interjected.

"And a very bad choice I must add."

"We're missing the point here. I wanted these guys together because I feel it will take a concerted effort to get her back. Gabriel has a street background and knows how to deal with guys like this. He knows this element way better than any of us." I supported.

"Since when did you become such a fan of Gabe?" Chloe asked. I looked at Max but realized that all eyes were on me. Chloe wasn't satisfied in the silence, her look begged for answers.

"This is getting weirder by the minute. What does he have to do with all of this?" Carl asked. I could see things going to an ugly place so I tried to regain control of the situation. Carl was on the verge of being irate.

"In order to get Reecie back we all have to be on the same page."

"How is that? When you're reading from a different book. All of this is news to me. But its starting to make sense." Carl explained.

"Let me see if I can clear it up for you. Max received financial benefits to change her testimony to a crime she had witnessed that sent a gang member to prison. The family figures the statement would free the man." Maxine gave me a sheepish look of embarrassment but I had to relay the facts to Carl so he'd be on board. "The whole plan backfired when the judge cited her for perjury."

"And you went to jail for that, hence getting the bail money, which explains the robbery and that's where you came in to play, with all your street knowledge." Carl was piecing it together looking at all the players involved. "So since she went to jail, you felt the need to tail some gangsters, rob them for their money, drug money probably, then bail your friend out of jail, hoping these thugs wouldn't figure out that you stole from them? Unbelievable! All of you. If I wasn't looking at yall, I'd think you were out of your minds. You're the First Lady for Christ's sake."

"Yes, but I'm also a mother and a devoted friend and

I couldn't leave her in as time of need. I'm loyal like that."

"Loyal, huh?" Carl scoffed. "How are we gonna get Sharice back? Where's the money? Can't we just pay them?" He pleaded. His questions were coming at me like machine gun bullets.

"I have the money but its not that simple. Two of the men who are responsible for holding her are now detained by the authorities."

"Those were the guys in the courtroom? The Crawford's?" Max asked.

"Yes. Their threats didn't do anything but trap themselves and free you."

"I'm just glad my son works for the FBI and was able to acquire those recordings. They incriminated themselves." "This is all making sense now," Gabriel spoke up. "That explains why we were being followed, remember that Chloe?"

"Yeah we saw-------" Chloe started her statement but I interrupted her when my phone lit up with an UNKNOWN number. Usually I don't answer those but we were on alert for any signs that would lead us in the right direction.

"If you want to see your precious daughter alive again, you need to get that money up!" My heart sunk hearing his demand. I wondered how he got my number but that was the least of my concerns. We were closer than ever so I had to play it right.

"Where is she? Where are you keeping my daughter?" The faces of everyone around me quickly turned to panic when they heard that. Instantly they knew the call was serious. Gabriel motioned for me to give him the phone, instinctively I gave it to him. He put the phone to ear and just listened.

"I have her in a safe place, somewhere dark and quiet where the rats can keep her company. I'll call this number in one hour to tell you where to meet. We can do an exchange, my money for your little girl." He handed the phone back to me but there was no one there.

"He hung up! How are we supposed to know what to do?"

"I just needed to hear his voice, its Rico." Gabriel said confirming who the caller was.

"How do you know?" Carl questioned suspiciously.

"Let's just say I've had a few run ins with him in these streets. Our paths have crossed with him coming out on the losing end. I'd know his voice anywhere, I know him and how he moves. He's a scared, dangerous guy but he won't hurt Reecie."

"Why you think that?" I asked.

"He's desperate for money probably because his uncle and cousin aren't there to back him up. The Crawford's are all a family and depend on each other."

"That all sounds good but how does that help us get her back?" Carl was getting impatient with all this planning and no action and I didn't blame him.

"He's predictable. As I said, I know his moves, I know how he thinks. He says he will call back in an hour to give us a meeting spot. We need to have the money ready to go by then so we can do the exchange. Money for Reecie."

An uncomfortable silence moved over us. I had the money stashed away in the house in a spot I knew no one would look. After the $10,000 I gave Gabriel for his participation and the $25,000 I used for Max's bond, I had $50,000 left for a rainy day. Well, I see the storm clouds forming.

While everyone sat in the living room quietly, I went upstairs to our bedroom. Carl and I both have our own walk in closets, instead of hiding the money on my side, I went to his. In the back, behind his fur coat and leather trench he never wears there was a chest with a lock. It had been broken for as long as I can remember. I went and bought a new combination lock then put the money in a black gym bag with "Fitness World" stamped on the side. He would never think to look there even if he knew there was money in the house. For one, Carl hasn't been to the gym in years and two, the chest contained some items from his past, things he wanted to stay buried.

The call came through one minute after the hour. We were all antsy yet relieved at the same time. The waiting was driving us mad.

"I got your money, where can we meet?" I asked with everyone listening intently.

"Meet me at High Bridge Park in Bowie. Bring the money and come by yourself."

"I think her father has a right to come with me. I don't think there's a herd of elephants that would keep him from his daughter." There was a brief pause which meant he was giving it some thought.

"Fine. The good Pastor can come with you, but that's it. Nothing funny, or there will be consequences."

"What time?" I wanted this over as soon as possible.

"I'm leaving right now, I'll be waiting on you."

The phone went dead and my heart started beating through my chest. "We need to go now, Carl, me and you. The rest of you have to stay here. He said no one but Carl and I."

"Yall really shouldn't go there alone. He's a dangerous dude and you don't know what he's capable of." Gabriel warned.

"I'll take my chances. I don't want him doing anything to Reecie."

"Well just be careful." Gabriel said. "But I'll have eyes on you."

Without another word, Carl and I shot out the door on our quest to get Sharice. The ride to Bowie would take us about twenty minutes, there was silence the entire trip. I'm sure he had a myriad of emotions as did I. The black bag of money rested in my lap, which I would gladly exchange for my child. I just hoped she was safe.

Carl pulled the Mercedes into the tree lined entrance of the park. An elementary school was right up the street so there were kids filtering around on the grounds. Nothing seemed unusual as we slowly rode over the gravely surface. It was still day time so there was plenty of light to see anything out of the ordinary. A few cars were parked not too far from each other. Parents with their children were playing by the merry-go-round, others were shooting hoops on an asphalt basketball court.

We parked, sat, and kept looking for a vehicle that could possibly have Reecie in it. Finally, I couldn't take it anymore, I got out and made myself visible. After a few moments a young man approached out of nowhere, walking towards a brown mini van with paneling on it. For a second, I discredited him for another pedestrian until he slid the door open revealing its insides. There she was, eyes wide open, mouth, feet, and hands bound with white ties.

When he snatched her out by her arm forcefully and put a gun to her head, I couldn't breathe. He was shielded by the van and another car so no one could detect any wrong doings. Carl appeared by my side and raised his voice louder than I've ever heard.

"Hey man, you don't have to do that. Put the gun down, we have your money." He tried to reason.

"Yeah here it is." I said as I reached into the front seat and pulled out the bag. He needed to see that we were serious because it was obvious he was. I opened the bag and showed its contents an approached him slowly.

"Put it there by that car then step away." He ordered. I did as he said trying not to agitate him, he could have an itchy trigger finger. As I backed up slowly towards our car, I saw a figure easing up behind the mini van. Rico was so focused on the money, he left Reecie unattended. I guess he felt safe knowing he could see us and

Reecie was behind him. Then, in a flash two objects projected through the air, attaching themselves to Rico's skin. Instantly, he started to shake and convulse uncontrollably. Holding the taser was Gabriel. Rico fell to the ground and rolled over on his back, feet in the air looking like a roach.

"G...G....Game? What.......t.......t..you....doing? He couldn't finish his sentence for all the voltage and quivering and slobbering. The gun dropped from his hand next to the open bag of money.

"Yeah, nigga, its me, your worst nightmare. This time I'm on the right side of the law. I get to look you in the eyes when they cart your sick ass off and charge you with kidnapping and extortion. Mr. and Mrs. Andrews, the police are on the way, if I were you, I'd grab that bag and make it disappear before they get here." I looked and saw Chloe untying Reecie, giving her a huge loving hug. Both Carl and I nearly knocked each other over trying to get to Reecie. Our whole family was still engaged in a group hug when the police arrived. By now, a crowd had formed watching them haul Rico into the backseat of the squad car.

The ride home was bitter sweet. I could see Reecie weeping in the back seat, being consoled by her big sister. I was overjoyed and sorrowful at the same time watching her. I knew she had been through something traumatic and as a mother there was nothing I could do to protect her. That's the most helpless feeling in the world. As a whole, our family has suffered through some trying times. Its a wonder how we'll make it through. At least we have 50,000 ways to help our wounds heal.

When we pulled up to the house, Gabriel was behind us like our guardian angel. Carl got out and walked over to him, extending his hand. "Thank you, young man. You definitely stood up for my family today. I'm indebted to you for your bravery."

"It's nothing. I did what any man would do for the ones he loves." He answered

"You are wise beyond your years. We could use your guidance down at the church with our youth ministry. I could set up something."

"Daddy!" Chloe chimed in. "Stop talking him to death." Carl just chuckled at his oldest. Having his family back together made him the proudest man alive.

"I'll swing you home if you would like" Gabriel offered to Max who had stepped out when she saw us arrive. The whole situation seemed to bring everyone closer. Drama can go both ways, it can build up or tear down. I looked at Carl and I could tell he has been worn down by everything that's transpired. But through it all, the happiness peeked through the dark clouds like sun rays.

"You OK?" I asked noticing his joy.

"Yeah, I'm good now. Could be better if you'd keep your hand out of the cookie jar." I had to chuckle. I deserved that one.

"I can make a mess when I want to." I retorted.

"Messy should be your middle name after this whole ordeal."

"I had no clue it would get this crazy, but hey, I guess that's how the cookie crumbles." I joked. He laughed too.

"At least we are all together, that's all that matters. I hope that doesn't change for a while."

I was about to comment when an Uber car stopped in front of our residence. We weren't expecting anyone, in fact Gabriel and Max were just about to leave. A young man got out of the car and looked in our direction. As I got a better view of him my heart found the beat of a thumping bass drum. It couldn't be him. With so much going on I completely forgot I told him to look me up when he got out.

"Cookie what's up?" Adrian was out. In the flesh. Standing on the lawn, a few feet away from me and my husband. Nothing was said because the whole scene was awkward. I smiled through it but didn't want to show how pleased in was to see him. He looked good, a lot better on this side of the fence. Carl had a sour scowl on his face but he wanted to see how I was going to handle it. With all the snooping and investigating he knew exactly who he was.

"Well, are you gonna introduce me to your boyfriend? Or are you going to leave him there looking as stupid as you're looking now."

Adrian sensed the tension into the air and took the high road. He turned and got back in the car sparing me and himself an uncomfortable encounter. It was probably for the best. He needed to move forward and live his life and I needed to pick up the pieces in mine.